The Last Lone Wolf

MAUREEN CHILD

First published in Great Britain 2011
by Mills & Boon, an imprint of Harlequin (UK) Limited,
Large Print edition 2011
Eton House, 18-24 Paradise Road,
Richmond, Surrey TW9 1SR

© Maureen Child 2010

ISBN: 978 0 263 21701 8

Harlequin (UK) policy is to use papers that are natural, renewable and recyclable products and made from wood grown in sustainable forests. The logging and manufacturing process conform to the legal environmental regulations of the country of origin.

Printed and bound in Great Britain
by CPI Antony Rowe, Chippenham, Wiltshire

MAUREEN CHILD

is a California native who loves to travel. Every chance they get, she and her husband are taking off on another research trip. The author of more than sixty books, Maureen loves a happy ending and still swears that she has the best job in the world. She lives in Southern California with her husband, two children and a golden retriever with delusions of grandeur. Visit Maureen's website at www.maureenchild.com

To Rosemary Estrada—

A great neighbor,
a good friend and the mother of
the four nicest girls I know.

This one's for you, Rose.

One

"Now *that* looks like trouble." If there was one thing Jericho King could recognize, it was trouble. Fifteen years in the Marine Corps had given him almost a sixth sense—a sort of internal radar. He could spot potential problems coming at him from a mile off.

This particular problem was a hell of a lot closer.

Jericho squinted into the late afternoon sunlight and watched as a short, curvy woman with long brown hair bent over and reached into a neon-green compact car parked on the gravel drive.

"Still, not a bad view," the older man beside him muttered.

Jericho chuckled. Sam had a point. Whoever the brunette was, she had a great butt. His gaze moved over that behind and then down and along a pair of truly sensational legs. She was wearing a pair of bright-red, three-inch heels that, even as she stood there, were sinking into the gravel and dirt drive.

"Why do women wear those idiotic shoes, anyway?" Jericho asked, not really expecting an answer.

"Generally," Sam Taylor mused, "I think it's to get men to look at their legs."

"They ought to know they don't have to work that hard," Jericho told him with a slow shake of his head. "Well, we don't have time to deal with her today. So whoever she is, I'll take care of it fast. Bet she's looking for that day spa on the other side of the mountain. I'll get her straightened out and on her way."

He took a single step forward before Sam's voice stopped him.

"Y'know," he said, "I don't think she's lost. I think she's the one I talked to about the cook job. You remember, you put me in charge of hiring Kevin's replacement?"

"Yeah but, a *cook?*" Jericho narrowed his gaze on the woman, still bent over, rummaging around in her car as if looking to find a stray gold nugget. "Her?"

"If that's Daisy Saxon," Sam told him, "then yeah."

"Saxon. Saxon..." Knowledge slammed into Jericho hard and fast. Shifting a glance at his foreman, he asked, "Did you say Saxon?"

"Yeah, your hearing's still okay," his friend said, then added, "Why? What's the problem?"

What's the problem?

"Where would I start?" Jericho muttered as the

woman straightened up, turned and spotted him
and Sam standing on the wide, front lawn.

She clutched an oversize purse to her chest as
she stepped onto the lawn and headed toward
them. Her long brown hair lifted in the wind, her
dark brown eyes were locked on him and her full
mouth was set in a firm line of determination.

Jericho watched her as something inside him
stirred. He squelched the feeling fast. This
woman wouldn't be staying, he told himself. If
she was really Daisy Saxon, then there was no
place for her here. Hell, he thought, just look
at her. Was there ever a more *female* woman?
When women arrived at his camp, they were
dressed for it. Jeans. Hiking boots. This one
looked as though she'd just left an upscale mall.
She was soft and pretty and delicate. And delicate wouldn't last here on the mountain.

Not in Jericho's world anyway.

He'd hear her out, apologize about the job confusion, then send her on her way. It would be
best for everyone—especially her. She didn't

belong here. He could tell that much just by looking at her. It only took seconds for these thoughts and more to rush through his quickly overheating mind.

"Pretty thing," Sam mused.

Jericho didn't want to notice, but damned if he could seem to help it.

The woman took maybe four uneven strides in those stupid heels before she tripped on a sprinkler head and went sprawling, sending her purse flying.

"Damn it." Jericho started for her.

But in the next instant, a tiny, furry creature jolted out of her purse and charged him with all the enthusiasm of a rabid pit bull. The grass was high enough that all Jericho could see of the miniature dog was its reddish-brown ears flapping in the wind.

Yips and barks in a pitch high enough to peel paint shot through Jericho's head as the improbably small dog, teeth bared, did its best to intimidate.

It wasn't much.

Sam's laughter erupted from beside him and Jericho muttered, "Oh, for God's sake."

Then he gently eased the mutt out of his way with one foot. The dog stayed on him though, even as Jericho neared the fallen brunette, who was already pushing herself up off the lawn.

Her hair fell in a tangle around her face. There were grass stains on the front of her shirt and disgust written on her face.

"Are you okay?" he asked, bending down to help her up.

"Fine," she murmured, taking his hand and staggering to her feet. "Nothing like a little humiliation to bring color to a woman's cheeks." Bending down again, she scooped up the little yapper. "Oh, Nikki, honey, you're such a brave little peanut. What a good girl, protecting Mommy."

"Yeah, she's a real killer."

"Mommy" now flashed him a look no friendlier than the one her tiny dog was shooting him. "She's very loyal. I appreciate loyalty."

"Me, too," he said, staring down into brown eyes that shone like fine whisky held up to a light. "But if you're looking for protection, you might want to upgrade to a real dog."

"Nikki is a real dog," she told him and cuddled the little creature close. "Now, I realize I haven't made the best impression in the world, but I'm here to see you."

"Do I know you?"

"Not yet," she told him. "But I know you're Jericho King, right?"

"I am," he said flatly and watched as her gaze slid back to his.

"Nothing like making a fabulous first impression," she whispered, more to herself than to him. A moment later, she lifted her chin and said, "I'm Daisy Saxon. We haven't spoken, but you wrote to me a year ago after..."

"After your brother died," he finished for her, remembering that moment when Brant Saxon had died following a dangerous mission into hostile territory.

Jericho had seen men die before. Too many over the years he'd served in the Corps. But Brant had been different. Young. Idealistic. And dead way before his time. The kid's death had hit Jericho hard, precipitating his retirement and leading him here, to this mountain.

The fact that he blamed himself for Brant's death only added to the misery he felt now, facing the man's sister.

Pain whipped through her eyes like a lightning flash. There and gone again in a moment. "Yes."

In an instant, Jericho saw Brant Saxon, remembered the fear on his face that had faded into resignation, acceptance, as he lay dying. And Jericho remembered the kid wresting a promise from him. A promise to look after Brant's sister if she ever asked for help.

Well, he'd done his best to keep the promise, hadn't he? He'd written the more "official" sorry-for-your-loss letter, then he'd called her later, offered to do whatever he could. But she'd turned him down. Politely. Completely. She had thanked him for his call, told him she would be fine, then she'd hung up—ending, as far as Jericho was concerned, any responsibility he'd had to her.

Until now.

So why in the hell was she on his mountain a year after telling him thanks but no thanks?

"I know a good bit of time has passed since we spoke," she was saying and Jericho tuned back in. "But when you called me, after Brant died, you offered to help me if you ever could."

"Yeah," he said, folding his arms over his chest. "About that. I never heard from you, so…"

"It's taken me a while to come to terms with Brant's death," she admitted, then sent a quick glance around her, checking out the property and Sam, still standing on the lawn watching them. "Could we talk about this inside maybe?"

Irritation spiked inside him and was instantly squashed. He didn't want to owe her but he knew he did. He'd given his word, not just to her brother, but to her. And one thing Jericho King never did was break his word. So he was going to have to deal with her whether he was happy about that or not.

He looked at her as she stood there, shivering a little in the cold wind blowing through the pines. Didn't even know enough to wear a jacket in the mountains. Even in California, fall could be a tricky time of year in the higher altitudes. But, he told himself, she was clearly not an outdoors kind of woman.

Of course she wanted to be inside. It was where she belonged. She was the kind who liked the great outdoors…from the other side of a window while sitting beside a fire and sipping a glass of wine. He knew her kind of woman all too well. And as he realized that, Jericho acknowledged that maybe he wasn't going to have to chase her off at all. Maybe she'd come to her senses on her own and admit that she wasn't suited to working here.

Besides, he could give her a cup of coffee at least before sending her off. Let her get a good look at the place she wanted to be a part of. See that she wouldn't like it. Wouldn't fit in. Wouldn't last.

"Sure. Let's go inside."

"Thanks," she said. "It's really cold here. When I left L.A. this morning it was seventy-five degrees."

"We're higher up," he pointed out dryly. Then he picked up on what she said. "You left this morning? And you're just getting here? At most, it's a three- or four-hour drive with traffic."

She rolled her eyes, planted a kiss on top of her silly dog's head and shrugged. "There was lots of traffic, but the truth is, I got lost."

Jericho just stared at her. "Didn't you have a GPS?"

"Yes," she said with a small sniff. "But—"

"Never mind." He turned, waved Sam off and

led the way toward the house. When she didn't fall into line beside him, he turned back to look at her. "What's the problem?"

Scowling, she jerked her leg and said, "My heels sank into the lawn."

"Of course they did." He walked back to her and said, "Step out of them."

When she did, he snatched the shoes up, handed them to her and said, "This kind of shoe won't work here."

She followed him, hurrying barefoot across the grass. She caught up to him, balancing the dog-filled purse in one hand and her shoes in the other. "But they look good," she told him.

"How'd that work out?"

"Well," she said on a half laugh, "it's a first impression you won't forget."

Jericho felt a short dart of admiration course through him. She wasn't easily shot down. Then he stopped and looked down at her. Her cheeks were pink, her eyes were flashing with humor and there was a smudge of dirt on the tip of her nose.

She was way too beautiful.

"What?" she asked. "Do I have dirt on my face?"

"As a matter of fact..." He bent, scooped her up into his arms and heard her "whoosh" of surprise.

"Hey, you don't have to carry me."

"Those heels wouldn't work on the gravel either, and you're barefoot, Ms. Saxon."

She packed a lot of curves into her small body. As she wiggled in his arms, he felt a reaction that surely would have happened to any red-blooded, breathing male. The problem was, he didn't want to react to her. All he wanted from Daisy Saxon was her absence.

"Right. Got it. Heels, bad. I'll remember. And call me Daisy," she told him. "After all, since I'm snuggled in against your chest, no point in being formal."

"I suppose not," he said tightly, as a small,

low-pitched growl erupted from the dog she held close. "That's a ridiculous dog," he muttered.

She looked up at him. "Brant gave her to me just before he shipped out."

"Oh." Well, hell.

He ignored the dog's warning growls and Daisy's stream of chatter about the house, the grounds, the weather, the fact that her car was almost out of gas and the nice people she'd met at the spa when she was lost.

His ears were ringing by the time he reached the front door of the main house. For a man used to the gypsylike life of career military, even owning a home was different. This place, though, was special.

This place had been in his family for almost a hundred years. One of his long-ago grandfathers had built the original cabin, then later it had been expanded into the King family getaway. Jericho and his brothers had spent nearly every summer of their childhoods here at the lodge.

It sat high on the mountain, square in the

middle of several hundred acres of forest, streams and rivers. The cottage had grown into a veritable castle constructed of logs and glass, blending in so well with its surroundings, it practically disappeared into the surrounding woods. It was a sort of camouflage, he supposed, which was something he was all too familiar with.

He'd bought out his brothers' shares of the place years ago and, knowing even then what he would eventually do with the place, had hired an architect to make some changes. The building had been expanded yet again, becoming at last a sort of fantasy mansion, with sharp angles, a steep roofline and enough rooms that Jericho never needed to run into a soul if he didn't want to. He'd had the work done before he left the Corps so it would be ready for him. When he left the Corps, Jericho had headed straight here.

This place was both a touchstone to the past and a foothold on his future. He opened the arched, dark wood door, stepped inside and set

Daisy on her feet quickly. Best to get that curvy body away from his as fast as possible.

She slipped her heels on and did a slow turn, taking in what she could of the house from the foyer.

"Wow," she whispered. "This is really..."

Cathedral ceilings arched high overhead, with pale, varnished logs crisscrossing in geometric patterns. The last of the afternoon sunlight slanted through the glass and lay dazzling golden patterns on the gleaming wood floors.

"Yeah, I like it." He led the way into the main room, right off the hallway, and she followed as he'd expected her to, those heels of hers clicking musically against the uncarpeted floors.

"It echoes in here," she said.

Jericho frowned as he looked back at her. "It's a big room."

"And practically empty." She shook her head as she glanced around. He followed her gaze. The furnishings were utilitarian but comfortable. There were sofas, chairs, a few tables and lamps and a long wet bar against one wall. There was a river-stone hearth tall enough for him to stand up in, and the view of the mountains was breathtaking.

"It looks like a barracks."

He shot her a look. "Clearly you've never seen barracks."

"No," she admitted, walking in, holding her dog and petting it as she moved, "but you've got this gorgeous place and it's decorated like…" She stopped and smiled apologetically. "Sorry. None of my business, is it?"

Jericho frowned again. What the hell was wrong with the room? No one else had ever complained. Then he told himself, city girl, and dismissed her observation entirely.

"So. Sam tells me you want to cook for us."

"Yes." She gave him a blindingly brilliant smile and Jericho felt that hard jolting punch of desire slam into him again. The woman was carrying concealed weapons.

"About that…"

Daisy saw the hesitation in Jericho King's ice-blue eyes. There was regret there, too, and she knew that he was about to turn her down. Destroy the plan she'd come there to set into motion. Well, she couldn't let that happen, so before he could say anything else, Daisy started talking.

"I spoke to Sam, your foreman. Was that him out front?" She carried Nikki with her as she crossed the room to stare out the wide front windows. She kept talking as she walked. "I should have said hello, oh, he probably thinks I'm a crazy person, showing up and falling flat on my face."

She didn't look back at Jericho. Couldn't afford to. Not yet.

He'd unsettled her. He looked so big and gorgeous and, well, grim. Probably didn't smile much, she thought, which might be a good thing because he'd affected her so much glowering at her, one smile might have done her in completely.

Funny, she hadn't expected this. Hadn't thought that one look at him would start her insides burning and her heart galloping madly in her chest. He was so tall. So strong. When he'd swept her up into his arms, it had been all she could not to sigh at him.

She'd chosen Jericho because of the bond he'd had with her brother. She hadn't expected to feel such an immediate attraction to the man. But that was good, wasn't it? At least, for what she had in mind it was a good thing. All she had to do was find a way to keep him from sending her packing before she did what she'd come here to do.

After all, she couldn't get pregnant with Jericho King's child if she wasn't here, now could she?

Two

"So," Daisy asked, plastering a confident smile on her face, "When do I start?"

She watched him watching her and yet, whatever he was thinking at the moment didn't show in his eyes. Those pale blue depths were shuttered, effectively closing her out. But that would change, she thought. Given a little time, she'd bring him around, win him over. Judging by the look on his face, though, that wouldn't be easy.

"Ms. Saxon—Daisy," he corrected before she

could say anything. "I've been out of town for the past few days. Sam told me only a few minutes ago about you applying for this job."

"I wasn't trying to keep it a secret," she said, meeting his gaze directly. "I mean, you offered to help me after Brant, but I didn't want to use that offer to get this job. I wanted to earn it on my own merits, you know? I didn't want you to feel obligated or anything, so I went through Sam when I heard about the job opening." Which was true, she thought, though she had counted on the fact that Jericho would feel obligated enough to keep her on once she was here. "I'm a very good cook, by the way. Sam saw my references and my résumé. When we spoke, he said he thought I'd do fine here."

"I disagree," he said tightly, and Daisy geared up for battle. "The fact is, I don't think you working here is a good idea at all."

Daisy swallowed hard. She really hadn't counted on this. Frankly, she'd expected Jericho to sort of go along with the idea. The whole obligation thing. He had once promised to help if he could. And her late brother had idolized the man. Somehow, she'd expected the "great Jericho King" to be just a bit more understanding. Well, he might not want her to stay, but she wasn't gone yet.

"Why not?" She threaded her fingers through Nikki's dark red hair so he wouldn't be able to see her hand shaking. But even as nerves rattled around in the pit of her stomach, Daisy told herself to get a grip. She wasn't going to let him see she was nervous. Wasn't going to acknowledge that even to herself. Not again. From here on out, it was affirmations. Focus on the positive. See the goal and get it.

With those thoughts and a dozen others just like them rushing through her mind, Daisy lifted her chin and waited for him to speak. Whatever excuse or reason he gave her, she was going to counter it. She would fight to be here. To stay here. To accomplish her goal.

To do that, she was going to show him just

how much he needed her here. How much she could bring to him and to his camp. And she was going to start right now. She had the element of surprise on her side.

"This place isn't like the spa you saw today in your travels across the mountain."

"You can say that again," she noted, turning a glance to the beige sofas and chairs. "Honestly, do you have something against color?"

"What?"

"Beige," she said, waving one hand to indicate the furniture in the room. "Beige isn't a color. It's the absence of color."

"Actually," he said, "that would be black."

"Well, beige is close," she insisted. "When you're running a place like this, you shouldn't go for industrial chic. You should have warmth in this room. And a few throw rugs would cut down on the echo."

"I don't mind the echo."

"I'm guessing the meals you serve your guests are as imaginative as the décor."

"I don't have décor," he pointed out.

"That's what I said."

"I meant," he said through gritted teeth, "I'm not interested in making this place into a fashionable inn."

"Oh, I agree. That would be all wrong. After all, you're going for the whole manly Survivorman thing, right? It doesn't have to be fussy," Daisy countered, already seeing in her mind's eye how it could look. A few pillows, some colorful braided rugs, maybe some splashy paintings on a few of the bare walls. "You want your clients to be comfortable, don't you?"

"This isn't a vacation camp. People come here to learn skills. Leadership. They come here to pit themselves against the mountain and Mother Nature."

"And when they come back to the inn victorious you want them to still be roughing it?"

He inhaled sharply and Daisy thought maybe she'd gone a little far. So she backed up fast. "I'm not saying you should put up lace curtains or use chintz slipcovers. I'm just saying that making this room a little more…comfortable would go a long way toward making your guests feel at ease. Couldn't hurt to think about it, right?"

"How did we get onto this track?" he wondered aloud.

"We were talking about how good I'd be for your business," Daisy told him and shushed Nikki when she growled.

He spared a dark look for her dog before he met her gaze again and said, "No, I was telling you I don't think this is a good idea."

"But you're wrong," she argued.

"I don't think so."

"You haven't given me a chance at all," she said, fighting both the glint in Jericho's eyes and the flutter of nerves in her belly. "You don't even know me. Plus, you haven't tasted my cooking. You haven't tried my fried chicken or home-style scalloped potatoes or my fudge mountain cake—"

"This isn't about… Fudge mountain?"

Daisy grinned as his eyes narrowed thoughtfully. "It's amazing. I'll make it for you."

Jericho took another deep breath, and she was frankly astonished that his broad, muscular chest could expand even farther. The man really was huge. And yet, he didn't give off the kind of "danger" vibe she associated with very big men. There was something…quiet about him. And that something was very attractive.

"It's not that easy," he said.

"Oh, making the cake isn't easy, but I promise you it's worth the effort." She deliberately misunderstood him. Keep him off balance, she told herself. *He's not sure what to do about you, so keep him that way,* she told herself.

"The job, Daisy," he said, and waved her over onto one of the couches. "Offering you this job isn't that easy."

"Sure it is. You offer, I accept. Easy."

He took a seat on the chair opposite her and braced his elbows on his knees. "When Sam was telling you about the job, did he bother to mention the survival test?"

She blinked. "Survival test?"

"I didn't think so." He scrubbed one hand across his face. "You see, there's a policy here at King Adventure. All new hires have to spend the weekend on the mountain with me. They have to prove they can make it here. Prove they have some survival skills."

Daisy set Nikki down onto her lap and stroked the little dog's back. Her mind was racing and her stomach was churning. Survival? All she knew about surviving on a mountain was finding a good hotel with a nice fireplace and room service. Why in heaven should a cook have to prove herself in the wild?

Anxiety pumped through her system and her positive thoughts began to crumble like broken cookies. But even while doubts slapped at her, she knew she couldn't give up on her idea before she even really got started.

"No," she said, "I didn't know about that."

"See?" His voice was kind, his eyes shone with relief and the patient smile on his face only irritated her immensely. "It just wouldn't work out, Daisy."

"Well," she shot back, "it's not like you're going to drop me off in the middle of nowhere with a knife and a piece of string. Are you?"

One corner of his mouth lifted briefly. "No."

"Then I can do it," she said, covering her own doubts with a veil of confidence.

Now he simply shook his head. "No, you can't. Hell, you couldn't take a few steps across the lawn without falling on your face."

She flushed and felt the heat of it stain her cheeks. "That was an accident."

"And out in the forest, an accident like that one could kill you."

"Then I won't let it happen again," she argued.

"Damn it, why won't you listen to reason on this?"

"Because I need this job," she told him flatly,

fingers curled protectively around Nikki. "My roommate got married and I couldn't keep the apartment on my own. My old job was downsized when the owner hired his cousin's nephew as head cook and—" She broke off quickly because she wasn't about to beg. And she wasn't the kind of woman to go all weepy, either, using tears to get her way.

"It's been a rough couple of months," she said simply. "So when I heard about this job opening, it seemed perfect. It *is* perfect. And I think I should get the same chance to prove myself as any other employee here has had."

He pushed himself out of his chair and stalked a few paces off. Glancing at her over his shoulder, he said, "It wouldn't be easy."

"No," she agreed, already dreading being out in the great outdoors. "Probably not."

"Why are you so determined to do this?"

"I told you why," Daisy hedged. "I need the job."

"If you're that good a cook, you could work anywhere."

"I want to work here."

"Which brings me," he said tightly, "back to the original question. Why are you so determined to work *here?*"

She lifted her chin, squared her shoulders and said softly, "Because you knew Brant."

He rubbed his face again in irritation. "I know it's not easy, losing family."

"My only family," she corrected and hated that her voice broke on the words. "Brant and I only had each other. When he died, I was alone. And I don't like alone."

Which was the absolute truth as far as it went.

She couldn't give him the whole of it, now could she?

She'd already admitted that she really did have nowhere else to go. She had no one. Her brother, Brant, had been her only family. Daisy was completely on her own now. And she hated it. She watched other families and felt her heart ache. She watched mothers with their children and something inside her wept. Daisy really wanted love in her life again. But she didn't want another man.

No, thank you. She had both been there and done that and hadn't even gotten the T-shirt. She'd convinced herself a couple of times that she was in love and it had ended badly. She wasn't interested in risking another broken heart. She wouldn't set herself up for that kind of disappointment again. But she did want to love and be loved. She wanted to have a family again. To be part of something again.

She wanted a child.

That thought settled everything inside her. Nerves drained away, anxiety faded and a cool, calm feeling swept through her. Whatever she had to prove to Jericho, she'd do it—for the chance at family. She'd made a decision and now she was going to go through with it. But he couldn't know what was driving her. Daisy couldn't very well tell him that she'd chosen him to be the father of her child.

If she felt a quick sting of guilt over the idea of tricking a man into being a parent, she smothered it a moment later. It wasn't as if she was asking him to marry her. Or to even take an active role in the raising of their child. All she really needed from him was his sperm.

Which just sounds awful, she thought with an inward groan. But it wasn't as callous as all that. She'd chosen Jericho because of his relationship with her late brother. Because he had been close to the only family Daisy had had.

And because Jericho King and the Marine Corps had stolen her family.

They owed her one.

"I don't baby prospective employees."

"Baby?" Daisy flushed, as if he were reading the thoughts racing through her mind.

Scowling, Jericho clarified. "I meant, I won't make it easy on you."

"Oh." She laughed to herself, then shook her

head. "I didn't ask you to." Oh, boy, she thought wryly, she'd probably regret saying that. He looked tough and she could only imagine that whatever he put her through to "earn" her way in wouldn't be pleasant. But she'd made up her mind to come here. To make her dream come true. And nothing he could do or say would stop her.

"You're as stubborn as your brother was."

Daisy smiled fondly. "Where do you think he learned it?"

Damn it.

"I'm not asking for a favor," she said quickly, wanting to speak up for herself before he summarily dismissed her. "I'm applying for a job I happen to be perfect for. I'm a terrific cook, you'll see. All I'm asking for is a chance."

In his letters home to her, Brant had often mentioned that Jericho King had the best poker expression he'd ever seen. Brant had insisted that no one ever knew what Jericho was thinking.

Apparently, leaving the Marine Corps hadn't changed that about him.

She didn't have a clue what his thoughts were. Hers were very clear, though.

She needed to stay here. She fixed a confident smile on her face, while Jericho King's blue eyes were locked on her. She wouldn't let him see that the thought of a survival test terrified her. Wouldn't let him know that she felt on edge. But everything she'd told him had been absolutely true.

His jaw went so tight she could actually see the muscles in his cheeks twitch. He wasn't happy with the situation, but he wasn't telling her to leave, so Daisy took that as a good sign. She pressed her case. "I can promise you that you won't be disappointed by my performance as cook. I'm not asking for a handout, Mr. King."

"Jericho."

A good sign and she'd take it as such. Her

smile brightened. "Jericho, then. All I'm asking for is a job. I can do it. You won't be sorry."

"No," he mused as he walked back toward her. "But you might be."

She huffed out a relieved breath. "Does that mean I'm hired?"

"Provisionally," he told her. "There's still the mountain test. I can't let you off the hook for that one. Every employee here has taken the weekend in the wilderness. You'll have to make it through, too. For now, I'll show you where you can stay. Let you get settled, then we'll head into the mountains in a couple of days."

Daisy held on to Nikki and pushed up off the sofa. Her first goal had been met. She was still here. And Jericho had no idea that once she had a foothold, she'd never let go. She knew exactly what she looked like—a helpless female. Well, looks could be deceiving, she told herself. She'd been on her own for years. She'd practically raised Brant on her own and she'd done a damn fine job of it, too. She could handle whatever

Jericho dished out and when it was all over and done, she'd still be standing. Plus, she'd have the right to be here, with the man she needed to help her rebuild her family.

She tipped her head back to look up at him and graced him with what she knew was a brilliant smile. "Thanks. Thanks for this."

"Don't thank me yet," he muttered and led the way out of the main room toward the staircase. "Before too long, I suspect you'll be cursing the day you ever drove up here."

Only, she thought, if she didn't get pregnant.

It was a hell of a thing, Jericho told himself, when a man was reduced to sneaking around his own damn house.

He'd never been a coward. Men he'd served with in the Corps would be willing to swear that there wasn't a damn thing in the universe that scared Jericho King. But here he was, avoiding one small, curvy woman as if she were Typhoid

Mary and he was the last healthy man on the planet.

She'd already settled herself in as if she'd been on the mountain for years. Her idiot dog was scrambling up and down the stairs, those tiny claws tapping against the wood floor until it sounded like a swarm of crickets had been set loose in the house.

Even the air was different, he thought. The faint trace of her flowery scent seemed to hang on the air, flavoring every breath he drew.

Jericho was on edge and he didn't like it. Hell, he'd arranged his life so that he dealt only with the people he wanted around him. After years of military living, he liked his privacy. Liked the fact that his clients came and went, hardly making an impact on his world at all. His employees knew when to back off and leave him alone, and when he needed a woman, he went out and found one.

Nothing permanent. Nothing lasting. Just a few good nights with great sex and some laughs.

That was the way he wanted it. The way he needed it.

Yet now, everything had changed. In the space of a few hours, Daisy Saxon was turning his world on its head. And he only had himself to blame. He could have turned her out on her pretty little ass. Hell, should have.

But truthfully, he hadn't been able to. The weight of what he owed her and her brother was still too heavy around his neck. Whispers of guilt, regret, slipped through his mind. If she knew the truth, she'd never have come here. So the only option for him was to agree to let her take the survival test on the mountain. Then she'd fail and leave and it wouldn't be his doing.

He went down the back stairs figuring to grab something to eat so he could avoid the whole sitting-down-to-dinner situation. There was plenty of work for him to do. Paperwork piled up because he tended to avoid it whenever possible. So he'd lock himself into his study with

a sandwich and avoid talking to Daisy until
tomorrow.

He slapped one hand to the door, pushed it
open and stopped dead. Damn it.

"Hi," she called out from her spot by the
stove.

She was wearing a pair of tight jeans, a yellow,
long-sleeved shirt and an apron that was so
large for her the strings were tied three times
around her narrow waist. Not only was she here
and cooking, whatever she had going smelled
great.

"What are you doing here?" He stepped
into the room and glanced around. "Where's
Kevin?"

"Oh, I told him I'd fix dinner tonight. He's
going into town to see his girlfriend."

Jericho scowled at that. Not only did she take
over his damn house, she started giving his employees the night off.

"You know, I didn't even realize you had a
town close by. Imagine that, I got lost for what

felt like hours and never saw the town?" She shook her head and laughed a little. "Must make it easier than driving all the way down the mountain when you need supplies."

He just stared at her. The woman talked more than anyone he'd ever known.

"It's not a problem that Kevin left for the night, is it?" she asked, watching him warily. "I only thought that since I'm going to be taking over his job soon—"

He narrowed his eyes on her. "That hasn't been decided yet."

"Oh, I know, but I believe in positive thinking."

"Uh-huh."

She smiled again. "Yes, I can imagine what you think of it, but affirmations can really make a difference in your life. Think it, be it, you know."

"What?"

She laughed again and the rich, throaty sound

rolled through the room and settled over him like a blessing.

"I just mean, you put out into the universe what you want to happen and it generally will."

"The universe."

"Sure. If all you do is think negative thoughts, then it's hardly surprising when you only experience negativity, right? So, same goes with the good stuff. Imagine you're happy doing exactly what you want to do and the universe will find a way to provide you with that dream."

He shook his head. "So the universe is going to help you through the mountain tests?"

"You bet!" She stirred the contents of a stainless steel pot on the stove. Instantly, even more unbelievably tantalizing aromas drifted into the air. "I'm envisioning myself succeeding and gracefully accepting your congratulations."

He smiled in spite of everything. She seemed so damn sure of herself. How were you supposed to argue with a woman who thought she could arrange her life simply by thinking?

The scent of whatever she was cooking reached him again and Jericho's stomach rumbled in appreciation, but he wasn't about to be seduced by a pot of soup. "You go ahead and keep imagining. I've got actual work to do. I'm just going to make a sandwich, then I'll be gone."

"Sandwich?" she said, and looked horrified at the notion. "That's not a meal for a man like you. I think we can do way better than that. Why don't you sit down and I'll fix you a snack that will hold you over until dinner."

He thought about refusing. He really didn't want to spend any more time around her than he absolutely had to. Especially if she was going to be spouting all of her New Age bull. But if he walked out now, she'd know he was avoiding her and he wasn't about to let that happen.

Instead, he walked to the high bar table at the back side of the cooking island and took one of the tall seats. He watched her as she pulled an oven door open and reached in with a hot pad to pull out a cookie sheet dotted with what looked like golden-brown half pies.

"This is an amazing kitchen," she was saying. "This warming drawer for instance. Keeps food hot but doesn't continue to cook them. And oh, my. The refrigerator shelf under the island—" She shook her head, patted her heart and sighed. "Keeps all of your vegetables right next to the sink and the cutting boards." She laughed a little and did a more dramatic sigh. "And I'm not sure, but I think I had an orgasm when I saw the Sub-Zero fridge." She caught herself, winced a little and gave him a sheepish smile. "Did I just say that out loud?"

"You did," he told her and wished he hadn't heard her. She said the word *orgasm* and his body went on red alert, instantly prepared to show her just what an orgasm should really feel like. At the very least, she wouldn't have had to wonder if she'd had one or not.

"Sorry," she said and walked to a cupboard for a plate. "I get a little emotional about great kitchens, and let me tell you, this one's a beauty!"

"Uh-huh." He didn't care. Until he'd hired Kevin to cook for them, the most the kitchen had seen was a lot of microwave action from him and Sam and the others who lived here. As long as the kitchen held a fridge for food and beer and provided a sink and ready fire, that was all he needed to know. Jericho remembered the kitchen remodel he'd done to the place years ago, but he'd simply turned the designer loose and hadn't asked any questions.

Their clients were served simple food and plenty of it. No one had ever complained. Now though, he gave it a quick look, following her pleased gaze. He took in whitewashed plank walls, dark cedar cabinets, dark green granite counters and a gleaming wood floor. There was an industrial-size cooking range, double ovens, a couple of microwaves and a refrigerator big enough to hold supplies for a battalion.

That wasn't even counting the two big freezers situated in the butler's pantry.

Overhead lights banished shadows, and through the wide windows on every wall, night was creeping its way across the mountain. Inside, though, the oversize room was feeling a little cramped at the moment.

She was standing just opposite him on the other side of the island. In front of her was more granite and a snaking stainless sink that served, as he recalled Kevin telling him once, as an "entertaining sink." Apparently, you could stock drinks in ice at one end of the sink, then as the ice melted, it simply drained away.

Didn't impress Jericho any. A cooler was just as good.

"You seem to have found your way around," he said finally, when he noticed she was simply staring at him waiting for him to say something.

"I have. It's like exploring an amazing new country." She slid open the refrigerated drawer, plucked something from inside and dropped it onto a plate beside a pie she'd already taken from the cooking tray. "Now, I want you to try this and I think you'll be glad I talked you out of having a sandwich," she said, sliding the plate across the counter toward him.

Jericho shifted his gaze from her to the plate and back again. "What is it?"

"It's *good*," she said, giving him a teasing smile. "Honestly, don't you have any adventure in your soul?"

"I've had plenty of adventures," he countered. "I just don't usually include food in them."

Still, he thought, it did smell good, not that he was going to admit it anytime soon. The half-a-pie was still steaming and alongside it sat a small bowl with a couple of radish roses, curls of carrot and celery beside a small dish of what looked like ranch dip. He lifted his gaze to hers. "Raw vegetables? Not a favorite."

"I'll make a note," she said with a shrug. "But for now, you could eat them anyway. They're good for you." Then she waved at the plate. "Try the pasty."

"Pasty?" One eyebrow lifted. "Not the definition of pasty that I'm familiar with."

It took a second to register, then she blushed—actually blushed, for God's sake—chuckled and that soft sound rippled through the room. "I can imagine. But *this* is a meat pasty. They're from Cornwall, originally, I think. Some say it pah-stee," she said. "Wives made them for miners' lunches. They were easy to carry and hold and satisfying enough to take care of a hardworking man's hunger."

Jericho nodded absently as she talked. Picking up the half pie, he sniffed it again, almost suspiciously, then took a bite. The piecrust simply dissolved in his mouth and the filling was... He groaned.

Daisy gave him a bright smile. "You like it!"

"You could say that," he muttered around another mouthful. He really hated to admit it, but she was a hell of a cook. "It's great."

"I'm so glad. I made them to go along with the homemade soup. I know soup isn't a very substantial meal, but with the fresh bread and the pasties…"

He held up one hand. Clearly extreme measures were needed if a man was going to get a word in edgewise. "You made fresh bread?"

"It's just a couple of loaves of quick bread." She sounded almost apologetic. "That way I didn't have to wait for the yeast to rise."

"Right." She'd only been here a few hours and she'd made soup, bread and this incredible pie he couldn't stop eating. Kevin was a good enough cook, but he didn't have half the drive this one small woman did. Plus, he wasn't exactly adventurous with his cooking, which was, frankly, one thing Jericho had liked about him. But, if this pasty of hers was any indication, he had a feeling "adventures in food" was going to be a good thing.

And, he had to admit, she might look like a flighty little thing, but she sure as hell wasn't afraid to work. She'd done more in a couple of hours than Kevin managed to do in a day. To be fair, Kevin probably would have enjoyed doing more, but cooking for a bunch of men probably sucked the creativity out of him. Daisy was still fresh enough that she was excited about her work.

While she talked, Jericho nibbled on the raw vegetables, surprising even himself. He'd always been more of a meat-and-potatoes man by choice. And frankly, being in the military had pretty much flattened his taste buds long ago. Food there was fast and plentiful. Cooked to keep a man on his feet, not to have him lounging around a table tempting his palate. But whatever kind of dip this was she'd concocted for the vegetables was damn tasty and the pie was good enough it could bring a grown man to his knees.

As if she could read his mind, she wagged her

index finger at him and said, "You'll like my soup, too. Soups are actually one of my specialties, which will work out really well up here during the winter."

"What kind of soup?" he grudgingly asked, since he was being tempted by the satisfaction filling his stomach at the moment.

She turned around, went back to the stove and lifted the lid on the pot again. Steam rushed up, carrying an amazing scent. "It's beef and barley. I found all of the supplies in the fridge and the pantry and it's so brisk and cold out right now, I thought soup would be good for tonight."

"It'll be fine," he said, already looking forward to sampling it as he finished off the pasty and wished he could get another one.

"I have got great recipes for tomato soup and chicken and leek—"

"Leek?"

She glanced at him. "You'll like it, I swear."

He probably would, he thought and warned his stomach not to get used to the good life.

"Anyway, when it snows up here, there'll be lots of good, hearty soups and breads and stews. Then in summer, you'll love my barbecued chicken wraps and—"

He cut her off before she could get too wound up. "Don't be making long-term plans just yet."

"Affirmations, remember?" she countered with a grin. "As for dinner, I'll do even better tomorrow night. What would you like? Pot roast? Pasta? Chicken enchiladas? Do you have any favorites?"

God, his mouth was watering just listening to her. Between her looks and her abilities with a stove, she was definitely double trouble.

Then she stopped and whirled around to look at him. "Better—what do you *hate?*"

A reluctant smile curved his mouth. Hell, he had to give her points for tenacity. He'd given her an inch and she was quickly scrambling to take the whole damn mile. He admired that in anybody. And for a woman alone, fighting to make a place for herself, it took even more guts to stride right in, settle herself and immediately go to work carving out her own niche.

But as much as she wanted this job, heck, as much as he'd like to get accustomed to eating this well, he couldn't let that happen. For her own sake.

And he almost regretted that fact.

Almost.

There's not much I won't eat," he finally admitted. "But we're not interested in anything fancy up here. I've gotten used to eating simple, plain food. Plus, it's better for the clients when they're here. Roast beef is going to give a man more energy on the mountain than a plate of snails."

"Ew. Snails." She smiled and shuddered. "No worries in that department, I promise."

"Okay, good." He finished off the pasty and thought about grabbing another as he watched her move around the kitchen. She sure as hell looked as if she knew what she was doing. Of course, he'd read her references, but tasting what she could do with food was different than reading about it.

He nibbled at the carrot and celery curls, dipping them in the accompanying sauce. She was a good cook, but that didn't mean she would make it here. Hell, he told himself, look at her.

His gaze locked on her, he noted her delicate but curvy build. Her hair was in a ponytail that swung back and forth across her back like a pendulum with her movements. She was humming something just under her breath and when she opened a cupboard and reached for something, Jericho was treated to a glimpse of very pale, very smooth skin displayed when her blouse hitched up.

His mouth went dry and his blood stirred. Damn, it had been too long since he'd indulged in a long weekend of sweaty sex. And now that *that* thought had taken root in his mind, he was picturing Daisy Saxon in his bed, that thick, soft hair of hers spread across his pillow. Her smile aimed at him as he moved in for a long, languorous kiss. Her breath sliding from her lungs as he entered her.

Instantly, he shut down that train of thought and squirmed uncomfortably on the bar stool. He didn't need her here. Didn't want her here. Couldn't have her here.

So he was just going to have to get rid of her—fast.

Three

"It's amazing," Daisy whispered, almost as if she were in church. She'd awakened early—too many years of getting up and moving in the restaurant business—and after getting dressed, she'd taken Nikki outside to enjoy the mountain quiet. Her little dog was off exploring the yard and all of the shrubbery, leaving Daisy alone in the shadows.

Now, she was standing on the lawn, staring back at the house and realizing that in the pearly

morning light, Jericho King's log and glass mansion looked almost like a fairy-tale castle.

She'd been too busy yesterday finding her
way there and then falling on her face to notice
much about the place. Her gaze swept over the
façade and another murmur of appreciation
slipped from between her lips. Wide balconies
stretched along the second floor, with arched,
twig-style railings. Behind those balconies,
glass panels soared, allowing views of the tree-
studded mountain and the lake in the distance.

The lodge itself was surrounded by tall pines,
and the wind whispering through the branches
sounded like sighs.

"It's a good place, all right." Jericho's voice
rumbled from right behind her and Daisy
jumped.

"I didn't hear you come up."

"I walk quietly. Tend to in the woods." He
stared up at the house as dawn painted the
honey-colored logs with rosy hues.

She nodded but silently guessed that his

stealthiness also came from so many years spent in the military. "Well, it's so quiet here anyway, it's as if you're afraid to make too much noise. I feel almost as if I'm in church or something. In the city," she said on a sigh, "there's always noise. Cars, trucks, sirens. Here...stillness."

"One of the things I like best about it," he said.

"I can see why," she agreed. "I get tired of the crowds and the hustle and bustle myself. Somehow everything always seems to be rushed down in the city. Being here is almost like being on vacation!"

"Except for the working aspect," he said dryly.

"Right." She nodded and then continued talking. "Anyway, I woke up early and decided to look around a little. I didn't actually get to see much yesterday and—" She broke off, looked up at him and added, "But I didn't see anyone else so I thought I was the only one up."

He laughed shortly, shoved his hands into the

pockets of a battered, brown leather bomber jacket and said, "Trust me, everyone's up." He turned and pointed across the wide compound at a smaller log version of the main house. "Sam and the guys live there and they've got a small kitchen outfitted so they can make coffee or whatever. You won't see them much in the mornings, but come lunchtime and at dinner, they'll be crowding around the table like they're starving."

"Good," she said, looking up at him with a determined smile. "I like cooking for people who like to eat."

"They do," he told her. "As for right now, they're all just busy doing the daily chores."

"Right. Of course." Foolish, she supposed, to have assumed she'd had the place to herself. But yesterday, all she'd seen was the main house and the barn. She'd never noticed the other building set back against the trees. Now she at least knew why the house had been so empty when she and Nikki had gotten up.

As if the thought of her had conjured the dog from thin air, Nikki barreled across the lawn, charging Jericho with a ferocity belying her size. Her low growl erupted from her tiny chest and when she reached them, she stood in front of Daisy as if daring the big man to hurt her.

Shaking his head at the dog, Jericho said, "You know that's just coyote bait."

She gasped, bent down and snatched up her dog. Cradling her close, Daisy stroked a hand down Nikki's back and shot a nervous glance around her at the surrounding trees. "Don't say that."

"Dogs like that don't belong here," he told her and his blue eyes were cold and remote. "Hell, it's small enough it could get carried away by a hawk."

"Great," she muttered, looking up. "Now I have to check the skies, too?"

"Wouldn't be a bad idea," he said, shooting the still growling dog a look of mutual dislike.

Then he shifted his glance to Daisy. "Why are you really here?"

"I told you."

"Yeah, but you could work anywhere. You're a good cook."

"Thanks!" She smiled at him and accepted the casually delivered compliment as if he'd delivered it with a speech and a glass of celebratory champagne.

"So why here?"

Daisy thought about that for a long minute. Wasn't as if she could tell him why…not exactly, anyway. So she did the best she could and walked a wide circle around the absolute truth. Setting Nikki down on the grass, she stood up and said, "I told you that I wanted a change…"

"Yeah, but this seems like a radical jump to make."

"Maybe," she admitted, taking another look at the fantasy lodge draped in sunlight, "but what's the point in making a change if it's a safe one?

If I just move from one apartment in the city to another? From one restaurant to another? That's not change. That's just...*ch*."

"What?"

"You know," she explained, "not a whole change, just a partial one, so a *ch*."

He shook his head again and rolled his eyes. "Why here, though?"

"Because you knew my brother," she blurted, giving him at least that much of the absolute truth. "And because Brant wrote to me about you. He admired you. A lot."

His features froze up and his eyes went glacial. Daisy had to wonder why.

"He was a good kid," Jericho said after a long moment or two of silence.

"Yeah," she agreed, "he was."

She'd come a long way in the past year. Used to be that thoughts of Brant would have tears filling her eyes and her throat closing up on a knot of emotion. Now, though, she could re-member him and smile. She drew on all of the happy memories she had of him to comfort her and the tears were coming fewer and further between these days.

Still, when she spoke about him, her voice went a little wistful. "He was several years younger than me, you know. Our parents died when he was very small, so I practically raised him. Always felt more like his mom than his sister."

"He told me about you."

"He did?" An eager smile curved her mouth. Oh, this was what she'd wanted. What she'd hungered for. Someone else who had known Brant. Who could remember him with her and keep his memory fresh and meaningful. Plus, Jericho King had known him at the end of Brant's life and those were pieces that Daisy needed. She wanted to know everything. "What did he say about me? No, wait." She stopped and held up one hand. "If he was complaining about me, maybe I don't want to know."

His features relaxed enough that one corner

of his mouth lifted. "Don't worry," he told her. "Brant only had good things to say about you. Used to tell his buddies all about your secret sauce for hamburgers. Talked about it so much he had the other guys begging him to shut up because he was torturing them."

"Oh, I'm so glad." Her eyes welled with unexpected tears and a too-familiar ache settled around her heart. "Thank you for telling me. It's hard for me, you know, not knowing what his life was like before he died. I mean, some of his friends wrote to me after…but it's really good to hear you talk about him. To know you knew him. And liked him. I— Damn it."

"Hey, don't cry." His eyes flashed and his voice was sharp. "Seriously. Don't."

She sniffed and huffed out a laugh. "I'm not going to. Oh, trust me, when I got word that Brant had died, I cried for days. Weeks."

Turning, she started walking because she just couldn't stand still a moment longer. Nikki was right on her heels as she moved across the lawn and Jericho was just a step behind the dog.

"It felt sometimes that I'd never stop crying. The slightest thing set me off. His favorite song playing on the radio. Finding his old first baseman's glove on the floor of his closet. Even Nikki made me cry."

"That I understand," he muttered.

Daisy laughed and was grateful for it. He was such a guy. "I meant, Brant gave her to me for my birthday just before he shipped out. So she was my last link to him and when he was gone—" Shaking her head a little, she sighed, looked down at the tiny dog and smiled. "But I realized after a while that Nikki was a blessing. With her, I wasn't completely alone, you know? I still had something from Brant with me."

"Yeah, I get that," he said softly.

She looked up at him, her gaze locking with his. "I appreciated the letter you wrote me."

His jaw worked as if he were chewing on

words to taste them before allowing them to escape. "And I'm sorry I had to write it."

"Oh," she said, giving him a tremulous smile as she reached out to lay one hand on his arm, "so am I. I wish with all my heart that Brant was still here. But he isn't. And I wanted you to know that it helped hearing from you. That reading about his friends and how much he meant to all of you gave me some comfort. You know, in case you were wondering."

He looked mortally uncomfortable and Daisy asked herself again, *Why?* Surely it would be a good thing for him to know that what he'd done had helped her get through a truly hideous slice of life.

"He was a good Marine," he said after a long moment of silence.

"High praise indeed, coming from you," she said, remembering all the letters Brant had written to her. "My brother talked about you all the time in his letters to me. About how he admired you. How he tried to emulate you. Learn from you."

Clearly unhappy with the conversation, Jericho bent down, snatched up a fallen twig from the grass and sent it sailing toward the tree line. "He did fine. Would have made a hell of a career Marine."

She knew that was exactly what Brant had wanted. Knew that her little brother had wanted to serve his country and test himself alongside other Marines. It had been important to him. So important that he'd given his life for his beliefs. And though her heart hurt still at his absence, being around Jericho—a man that had known and served with Brant—made it almost seem as if she hadn't lost him completely.

That was only one of the reasons she'd come here to get pregnant, she reminded herself. Jericho had known and liked Brant. But he was also a part of the very military that had taken the last of her family from her. Wasn't it only right that he now give her a family?

She winced at the direction of her own thoughts. She wasn't a woman used to lying or manipulating. And a part of her wasn't happy with what she was doing. After all, she was planning on tricking a man into making a child with her. Things didn't get much more devious than that.

But what choice did she have, really? She wanted a family again. Wanted to love again. And if she came right out and asked, she was sure Jericho wouldn't say, *Sure, let's get right on that!*

No, this was the only way. The only way to fill the hole in her heart left by Brant's death.

"You know," she said thoughtfully, "I almost met you before."

"When?"

"At Camp Pendleton. I went to see Brant before he shipped out and while he was show-ing me around the base, he spotted you." She smiled at the memory. Her brother had been so excited, so proud. He'd introduced Daisy to most of his friends and taken her to his favorite spots on base. "You were coming out of some building and Brant was dragging me over to meet you when a colonel walked up to join you. When the two of you left together, Brant was disappointed."

She also recalled clearly just how good Jericho King had looked in uniform. Tall and built and, even from a distance, clearly gorgeous. She'd been a little disappointed at not meeting him herself. Yet, here she stood now, more than a year later, at his home. *Life took you on some pretty strange journeys,* she thought.

"He was a good Marine," Jericho said again, as if struggling to give her whatever it was she needed to hear. "He had a lot of friends in the unit."

"He was always like that," Daisy answered with a wisp of sorrow in her voice for days gone past. "People liked being around him."

He nodded but didn't say anything. As they came to the edge of the lawn, the rising sun began to clear the treetops, spilling what looked like gold dust across the tips of the pines. "I liked your brother," he finally said, staring off down the mountain as if searching for signs of an invading army. "Because of that, I'm going to tell you something you need to hear whether you want to or not."

"Sounds ominous."

He tore his gaze from the distance and looked down at her. "You don't belong here, Daisy."

"What?"

She hadn't expected that, but looking at him now she couldn't imagine why not. Harsh shadows cast by sunlight sliding through the trees lay across his face, darkening his eyes and making him look even more formidable than usual. His mouth was a grim, straight line as he said, "You don't belong here, on the mountain. This is not your kind of place, Daisy."

Worry gnawed at her insides for a few uncomfortable moments, then that sensation gave way to aggravation. Was he going to change his mind? Toss her out before he'd even given her a chance to prove herself? He didn't know her. Didn't know what she might be capable of or not. How dare he think he could decide what she could and couldn't do.

"It's my kind of place if I say it is," she told him.

He blew out a breath and his mouth tightened even further until she could see that muscle in his jaw twitch again. "It's not that easy. Besides, I don't think your brother would want you here."

She blinked at him. Using her brother to get rid of her? "Excuse me?"

"You think Brant would be crazy about the idea of you living on a remote mountain top with a bunch of ex-Marines? Living with a bunch of guys isn't easy."

Former Marines? All of them? She shook that thought away and stayed focused on the conversation.

"Brant was a Marine. He'd probably love the

fact that I'm here. He'd consider me to be perfectly safe surrounded by the kind of men he trusted."

"You're making this harder than it has to be," he muttered.

"No," she told him flatly. "You're the one doing that. All I did was apply for a job. Which I got. You've already tasted my cooking and loved it. So the only complaint you've got against me is that I don't *belong* here? Not good enough."

She stared up into pale blue eyes that seemed to be boring directly into hers as if he were trying to read her thoughts before she could say them. "Now, I'll remind you that Brant was my *younger* brother. He didn't make decisions for me, and it would be really difficult for him to start doing it now."

Jericho King's scowl was an impressive thing. She imagined it had once frightened young recruits into jumping to attention and springing into whatever action Jericho had expected from them. She refused to be intimidated by it.

"I knew him," he pointed out. "I think I can figure out you being here wouldn't thrill your brother."

"Yes," she agreed, "you did know Brant and I'm glad to have that connection. Somehow," she added, "it makes his memory come more alive when I'm around other people who remember him. *But* I knew him better, I think, than you did. And even if he were here to cast a vote on all of this, it wouldn't be up to him. This is my decision."

"And mine," he reminded her.

His face looked hard and his eyes were as cold as twin blocks of ice. The rising sun spilled more light and created darker shadows all at the same time. She watched Jericho's face, hoping to spot a chink in his armor. But she found nothing. There was no give on his features, no soft understanding or kind consideration. This was the face of a warrior. A man tested in battle and honed down to a fine edge. If she expected to hold her own with him, she'd need every ounce of her own strength and self-confidence. If she let him know she was worried in the slightest, that would give him far too much of an advantage in this little test of wills.

She took a breath, blew it out again and said, "Okay, yeah. It's your decision, too. But you promised me a chance. And I'm holding you to it."

He blew out an impatient breath. "You've got to be the most stubborn woman I've ever met."

"If you think I'm insulted by that, you're wrong." Daisy bent down, scooped up Nikki and held her close. "Maybe I've never been on a battlefield, but I've had to work hard for everything I've ever had."

"That's not—"

"I know what it's like to push yourself." She cut him off neatly and poked him in the chest with the tip of her index finger. "I've been on my own a long time. I raised my brother by myself with no one to help. I know what it is to be so tired all you want to do is lie down and not get up for a year. And I know what it's like to ignore that urge because you've just got way too many things to do." She lifted her chin and fixed her gaze on his. "I'm not afraid. I'll do whatever's necessary to get what I want."

He nodded abruptly. "You know what? Fine. You don't want to listen to reason, that's your choice. You want to do this, we'll do it. Be ready at dawn tomorrow. We'll head up the mountain and then we'll see just how badly you want this stupid job."

He had to be out of his mind. That was the only explanation for any of this. In the soft, hazy light just before dawn, Jericho checked the sky, hitched his backpack higher and glared at the house. As if firing dirty looks at the place would make Daisy Saxon appear.

"It ain't dawn yet," Sam said as he walked up quietly.

No, it wasn't. So she wasn't late yet. "Close enough."

"Uh-huh." The older man shoved one hand through thinning gray hair. "So what's the plan, JK? You taking her out on the mountain just to submarine her?"

He shot one wary glance at his friend. Was he that easy to read? Would Daisy figure out that he was going to see to it that she failed her survival test? Besides, it wasn't as if he were going to deliberately sabotage her. He just wouldn't be offering her any extra help. And left to her own pitiful devices, he had no doubt she'd be finished before the day was out.

"What do you care?" he asked, neither confirming nor denying the man's suspicions.

Sam gave him a look Jericho hadn't seen since the older man had been his drill instructor when he first joined the Corps. When he was through with boot camp, Jericho and Sam had become friends and had kept in touch through all of their separate postings over the years. Sam had been a Marine for twenty years when he mustered out and coming here to King Mountain had seemed the logical choice.

The older man had been restless—too young to retire and too old to stay in the Corps—so he'd come here and become a part of King Adventure. He'd had as much a part in making the camp successful as Jericho had and they got along fine usually, two men with like minds, though they were separated by nearly two decades in age.

They were family, Jericho realized. But then, so were all of the guys who worked for him. Misfits mostly—men with no families, nowhere to go. Some had seen combat and didn't feel comfortable around lots of people. Some had simply yearned for wide-open spaces and a job with fewer restrictions than the nine-to-five route. Whatever their reasons, they'd all come here looking for work and wound up finding a place to call home.

And until this very moment, he and Sam

hadn't butted heads over anything important in years.

"She seems like a nice kid, is all," he was saying. "And I don't want to think you're taking her on the mountain just to break her spirit."

Jericho felt a rush of irritation swamp him as he looked at one of his oldest friends. The fact that guilt was riding right under that irritation was only more frustrating. Did the man have to read him so well? "Damn it, Sam, I would have thought you'd not only understand but agree with me on this. Did you get a good look at her? You can see for yourself she doesn't belong here."

He snorted and shoved his hands into his jeans pockets. "I see nothing of the kind. I see you trying to get rid of a pretty woman because she makes you twitchy."

Twitchy didn't even begin to cover what Daisy did to him, Jericho thought, but damned if he'd admit to it. "Bull. I'm doing this *for* her, not *to* her."

"Yeah, you can say that all you want, but

I've known you too long to buy into it." Sam shook his head and smiled knowingly. "That girl in there gets to you and you don't like it, so you figure to haul her ass out before she settles in."

Another shot too damn close to home, Jericho told himself and wondered if he'd somehow lost his poker face over the past couple of years of civilian life. Or maybe he was only transparent to people who'd known him so damn long. "It's not just that—"

Sam snorted again.

"Fine, you want me to admit it? She's hot. Hot enough that I've been on edge since she fell onto the lawn practically at my feet." He scowled into the distance, where the rising sun was just kissing the treetops. "Hell, she's a walking forest fire. But it's more than that. I served with her brother. Her *dead* brother. Now she's looking to me to provide a kind of link to him or something."

"That so bad?" Sam countered. "Everybody

needs connections, JK. She lost her brother. Isn't she entitled to whatever it is she can get from us? From you? Don't we at least owe her the straight-up chance at getting what she wants?"

Jericho really hated to be lectured. Especially when the lecturer had a point.

"I saw you at dinner last night," Sam went on, his voice a little lower, filled with what almost sounded like understanding. "And off the subject, the girl cooks a mean pot roast—but I saw the way you looked at her."

That's just great, Jericho told himself. He'd gone so far as to be fantasizing over a woman at his dinner table—and doing it obviously enough for others to notice. Just one more reason to get Daisy gone. His legendary control was clearly dissolving, which was something he would not put up with.

"Drop it, Sam."

"I'm not saying I blame you any. She's a pretty one. But if you're thinking she's one of your weekend types, you can think again." The older man narrowed his eyes. "That's a good girl. A nice one. And she deserves better than a quick roll in the hay and a one-way ticket off the mountain."

He knew that. Knew that Daisy Saxon had "complications" written all over her. It was just part of why he wanted her the hell away from him. He wasn't looking for complicated. He preferred simple.

"Sergeant Major," Jericho grumbled, "when the hell did you turn into a nanny?"

"I'm sayin' what I'm sayin'. And part of what I'm sayin' is that you owe that girl's brother better than to treat her badly." Sam glared at him. "You give her a real shot on the mountain, JK. See if she's got what it takes to make it here. And be honest with yourself about why you want her gone."

While Sam stalked off toward the two-storied barn several hundred yards away, Jericho was left to fume in silence. Been a long time since anyone had dressed him down like that and damned if he cared for it.

He made his own rules now. He hadn't answered to anyone since he left the Corps and he wasn't about to start now. Yes, he thought, he owed Daisy Saxon something because of her brother.

But was what he owed her a job? Or was it getting her back to the world she belonged in? Off the mountain. Back in the city. He was torn now. Undecided when before it had all seemed so clear. Maybe he *was* being too hard on her. Maybe he should give her a chance and just learn to live with his body's discomfort when he was around her. Maybe...

"We're ready!"

He turned to look at the back door of the house as Daisy stepped off the porch. He sighed. She looked great. And completely inappropriate for the hike they had stretching out in front of them. If he'd had any doubts a minute or so ago, they were gone now. She was very clearly not the outdoorsy type of woman.

Her hair was pulled into a long tail at the back of her neck. Her face was bright as a new penny and wreathed in smiles. She was wearing designer jeans with a red sweater and shiny black boots with a two-inch heel, and she had a duffel bag slung over one shoulder while she cradled her fake dog with her other arm.

Jericho sighed. Nope, he thought. He was doing the right thing.

She just didn't belong.

Four

Daisy was willing to put up with the back-pack Jericho had forced her to wear. She had even thanked him for the heavy jacket he borrowed for her from Kevin, the cook. She had dutifully changed into sneakers when he threatened to break off the sweet heels on her favorite boots. But she absolutely refused to leave Nikki behind.

"Everything's new to her, and she'll be afraid without me." She continued the argument even though he'd surrendered ten minutes ago. She glared at his broad back as he hiked five feet ahead of her through the trees.

He didn't even turn around to look at her when he said, "That dog has no business on the trail. She'll get eaten or lost or God knows what."

"No, she won't," Daisy insisted, snuggling Nikki's cheek to her own. The tiny dog's rapid heartbeat felt like the brush of butterfly wings against her palm. "I'll take good care of her."

"Unbelievable."

At least she thought that was what he muttered but she couldn't be sure. He was certainly grumpy on a hike. He didn't even seem to be charmed by the beauty all around them. Daisy was, though. Barely gone from the lodge, they'd been swallowed up in the thick woods and one look back over her shoulder assured her that she couldn't even see Jericho's home anymore. If he hadn't been with her, she'd wander through the forest for days without finding her way, which made her a little anxious. But a moment later, she dismissed the worry—since she *did* have Jericho—and gave in to her surroundings.

Her head swung back and forth as she tried to take in everything at once. The floor of the forest was spongy and soft, making her feel almost as if she were on springs when she walked. Layers of pine needles cushioned the ground and sent up a fresh scent every time she took a step. The trees all around her seemed to scrape the sky.

As they walked on, there was the occasional clearing where late-blooming wildflowers struggled to survive in the cooling weather. And then there was the sky. She didn't think she'd ever seen anything that shade of blue. Down in the city, there was so much smog and so many buildings, the tiny scraps of sky you could see were never that beautiful. It made even the relentless walking more enjoyable. When she fell, landing face-first on the cushiony ground, she could only blame it on not watching her step.

"Ow!"

Nikki jumped from her grasp instantly and

darted into the undergrowth before Daisy could call the dog back. Then Jericho was at her side in an instant, grabbing hold of the shoulder of her red sweater and pulling her to her feet in one smooth motion.

"Are you all right?"

"I'm fine," she muttered, more embarrassed than hurt. She brushed pine needles, dirt and who knew what else off the front of her sweater and the knees of her jeans. "I was watching the sky, and— Nikki honey, come back here!"

"Keep your eyes on where you're going, all right?"

"I will, it was just pretty and— Nikki!"

The dog barked from somewhere nearby and Jericho muttered a curse.

"I scared her when I fell," Daisy said in defense of her dog. "I think I tripped on a rock or something."

"You sure you're all right?"

"I'm fine. Just humiliated." The little dog raced toward her then and hopped on its hind legs as if doing a celebrational dance. "There you are, sweet girl! You scared Mommy running off like that."

"Mommy?"

"She's all mine," Daisy said with a grin as she bent down to attach a bright-red leash to the chest halter the little dog wore.

"Right." Jericho shook his head. "Can we go now?"

"Sure." She was determined to be upbeat and positive through this entire experience. She'd earn her place on this mountain if it killed her. "I'm sure I can walk another ten miles no problem. We've already come about that far, right?"

He raised one eyebrow. "We've gone about two miles so far."

"Really? Well, that's disappointing," she said, silently acknowledging the aching burn in her thighs and calves. "It really seemed longer."

"You're telling me," Jericho muttered, then started walking again. Daisy fell into step behind him, keeping one eye on the trail and the other eye on Nikki.

Though being at that altitude made talking, climbing and breathing all at the same time a little difficult, Daisy struggled on.

"I looked you up, you know, before I came here," she called out.

"Is that right?"

She frowned when he kept walking without so much as a glance at her. He couldn't have let her know any more clearly that he wasn't interested in what she was saying. But that didn't silence her.

"Well, not just you, but this place. The mountain itself. Did you know that grizzly bears used to live here?" Just saying that aloud had her checking the tree line warily even though she knew the animal was mostly extinct in California now.

"Yep," he said, "I knew."

"And," she added, "did you know that King Mountain is the largest piece of acreage bordered on wilderness area that's still in private hands?"

"Knew that, too."

She frowned and chewed at her bottom lip. Of course he knew, it was his land after all, but he could at least pretend to be polite about listening. "I saw a waterfall, too, on one of the maps I looked at. Are we going to see that on this trip?"

"Might."

Aggravating man, she thought as her temper began to simmer. He was deliberately not talking to her. Probably trying to make her be quiet by his lack of response. Clearly, he didn't know her very well. Her mother used to say that Daisy could talk to a stump. Which, she mused, she actually was doing.

"I still can't believe you own your own mountain," she said, shaking her head, as if trying to wrap her mind around it. "I mean, did you know your name is on actual maps? King Mountain."

"Yeah," he muttered, "I know. Did you know that you shouldn't talk so much on the trail?"

"Really? Why?"

He turned and glared at her over his shoulder. "There are wild animals out here. You might want to pay attention to your surroundings."

"But you're here."

"Yeah, I am…"

"What kind of wild animals?" she asked after a moment's pause in which she thoroughly scanned the surrounding tree line for any sign of slavering beasts hidden in the shrubbery. "There aren't grizzlies, I know, but…"

"There are still black bears. And brown bears," he said. "Not to mention coyotes, the occasional wolf and oh, yeah, mountain lions."

"Seriously?"

"Thought you researched the mountain."

"I did but—" Nowhere had she read about mountain lions. How had she not considered that?

"Still glad you brought that dog?" he asked.

Visions of Nikki being carried off by God knew what flew through Daisy's mind and she reined in the dog's leash as she hurried her steps to close the distance between her and Jericho. He might be surly, but he knew what he was doing out here and she was pretty sure he wouldn't let her or Nikki get eaten.

"More glad now than before," she told him when she was no more than an arm's reach from him. "She's better off with me. Where I can make sure she stays safe."

"And who's making sure *you're* safe?" he asked, shooting her a sidelong glance.

"That would be you," she told him, giving him a bright smile.

"I'm not here to help, you know," he said. "It's my job to be with you on this trail. But I'm here to see how you handle yourself out here. I'm the observer. The taskmaster."

"I know that, but—" They came around a sharp bend in the trail and Daisy stopped dead, conversation forgotten. "That's just gorgeous," she whispered, the words sliding from her on a breathy sigh.

She felt him come up right beside her. Felt the heat of him reaching out for her, felt the sizzle of awareness that ricocheted through her in response. But she didn't take her gaze off the picture in front of her.

A clearing. Knee-high grasses, spotted with deep-red wildflowers. And moving through it with a sort of balletic grace was a deer. As if it weren't quite real, the animal stepped through splotches of sunshine and dipped its great head to nibble at the grass. Caught in the moment, Daisy reached out, took Jericho's hand in hers and squeezed it, almost reassuring herself that she was really there. Really seeing something so beautiful and wild and perfect.

His long fingers wrapped around hers and he held on for a breathless moment and the two of them were linked—suspended in time.

Then Nikki barked and the deer lifted its massive head, looked directly at them, then bolted in the opposite direction.

As if the dog had spooked more than just the deer, Jericho dropped Daisy's hand and said brusquely, "We should get moving."

Her heart was pounding, thundering in her chest until she felt as if every breath was a battle. Her skin was still humming, as though his skin was still pressed to hers. The heat of his touch slipped inside her and Daisy folded her fingers into a fist, futilely trying to hold on to the sensation. When she could trust her voice, she asked, "Are we really going ten more miles?"

"No. Just a couple more before we make camp."

Though she was grateful, the thought of even two more miles made Daisy really want to whimper, but she controlled herself. She couldn't afford to look weak. Couldn't let him see that her legs were already aching and her shoulders hurt from the weight of the stupid backpack. She was going to prove to him that she could fit into his world, then she would be that much closer to what she wanted.

"Only a couple?" she forced herself to say. "What're we waiting for?"

One of his black eyebrows lifted into a high arch and he gave her a speculative look that hid as much as it said. But after another moment or two, he simply said, "Keep the dog quiet. Some animals won't be startled by it barking. They'll be curious. Maybe hungry."

She gasped. "You're doing that on purpose, aren't you? Trying to scare me."

"You should be scared, Daisy. This isn't a city park. This is the wilderness and the animals you'll meet out here aren't the kind you're used to seeing on TV or in the movies. They don't laugh and dance and they don't like people."

"I'm not an idiot," she told him. "I know that wild animals are just that. Wild. I also know I'm a little out of my element—"

He choked out a laugh at that one.

"But," she continued doggedly, "I'm going to do this."

He shrugged and walked off with long, lazy strides. "If you're bound and determined, then get a move on."

She tamped down the exasperation bubbling inside her and swallowed back a sea of retorts she wanted to hurl at his back. Then she realized that he was getting way too far ahead of her. So Daisy held Nikki a little closer and hurried to catch up to the man who was, at the moment, the very center of her world.

Why wasn't she making him crazy? Jericho asked himself for at least the tenth time in the past couple of hours. When he was out on the mountain, he liked silence. Sure, some of his clients were incapable of being quiet for very long at a stretch, but Daisy Saxon was in a class all by herself. The woman hadn't stopped her rambling conversations since they'd left the house.

She talked about the forest, about her former

job, her late brother and the boyfriend who had not only left her for her friend, but also had stolen her credit card on the way out the door. That story had just amazed him, though he hadn't commented. The man had to have been an idiot to walk out on Daisy, in Jericho's opinion, and she was better off without him.

And when she wasn't talking about her own life, she was pestering him with questions about his. She talked about the sky, what kind of music she liked best and how she planned to make him that fudge mountain cake of hers as soon as they got back to the lodge.

His ears had been ringing for hours and damned if he hadn't half enjoyed listening to her. She was interested in everything. Had an opinion on everything as well and wasn't afraid to voice it.

But in all the ranting, he acknowledged silently, she hadn't complained *once*. And that surprised him. It wasn't often Jericho was surprised by anything. So the fact that Daisy could make him rethink his original opinion of her was astonishing.

The last bunch of clients he'd had out on the mountain included a bank manager, who had prided himself on his rugged individuality, had wept like a baby after a few hours on the trail. He'd bagged the wilderness trip and called it quits as quickly as he could.

Yet Daisy, not a peep.

He knew she was tired. Her steps were less brisk and even her attempts at conversation were beginning to slow to a trickle. But she hadn't stopped. Hadn't asked to rest. Hadn't whined about a damn thing, and Jericho had to admit he admired her for it. She was more than he'd thought. But in the long run, did that mean anything?

She stumbled and, instinctively, he reached out and grabbed her elbow to steady her. Just touching her sent another zing of heat shooting through him, so he let go of her fast and when he spoke he was harsher than he should have been.

"Watch your damn step or you're going to break a leg or something and I'll have to hump you out."

"Hump?"

"Carry," he explained curtly.

She nodded. "Right. Sorry. I was watching Nikki."

"Let me watch the damn dog," he told her in little more than a growl. "You watch where you put your feet."

"Wow, King Crabby." She didn't wait for his response. "You really don't want me out here, do you?"

"I just think it's a mistake."

"Yes, so you've told me, but it's not." She turned her face up to him and a brilliant smile curved her luscious mouth. "And admit it, I'm doing better than you thought I would. Go ahead," she urged, "say I'm doing well."

He blew out a breath. "The fall notwithstanding, yeah, you've done all right so far."

"Thank you! What a nice thing to say."

He chuckled in spite of himself. She was still smiling and her eyes shone with humor and pleasure in the moment. She had to be exhausted and irritated with his behavior, but damned if she didn't keep her own spirits up.

"You're an odd one, aren't you?"

"Not odd," she corrected, "just different. For example, when someone else is crabby, I don't get crabby back. I try not to let their mood affect mine."

"Uh-huh," he said, picking up on her not-so-subtle jab. "That was a nice shot. You've got good aim."

"I know," she said, glancing at her dog to make sure the tiny thing was still in sight. "So how much farther?"

One dark eyebrow winged up. "Tired?"

"Nope." She lifted her chin and met his gaze. "I could go for hours yet. Just curious."

"Sure," he said with a shake of his head. "All right. Listen."

"To what?"

He sighed. "You have to be quiet to listen."

"Right." She snapped her mouth closed and frowned in concentration. After a moment or two her eyes slowly widened. "What is that? It sounds like hundreds of people talking in whispers."

"It's the river," he told her. "Just around that bend there, by the crooked pine. We'll set up camp there tonight."

She sighed heavily and he heard the unspoken relief in the sound.

Still, he had to give her points, if only internally. As close to the edge of collapse as she might feel, she wasn't letting him know it. The woman was running on sheer grit and determination. And that was something Jericho approved of. He even thought that maybe he'd dismissed her too easily, judging her by her looks and her clothes and telling himself that no one that pretty, that dainty, was made of stern enough stuff to make it in his world.

The problem was, he didn't want to be wrong about her. His life would be much easier if she just failed this little test and took herself back to where she came from.

By the time they made camp, Daisy was clearly exhausted, but worked right through it. She helped him lay out sleeping bags, then watched as Jericho set up a campfire ring. He set large rocks in a small circle, while clearing away any nearby brush that might catch with a stray spark.

When he was finished, he laid a couple more flat-sided rocks inside the ring and built a campfire. Once the flames were going, Daisy took over, surprising him again. She carried the battered tin coffeepot down to the nearby stream, filled it with water and set it on one of the rocks to boil.

"You almost seem to know what you're doing," he commented.

"Well, I was a Girl Scout like a hundred years ago," she said quietly. "I went on a couple of overnight trips and I can still remember watching our troop leader setting up camp." She flashed him a smile and in the firelight, her features were soft, ethereal and downright beautiful.

Darkness surrounded their campsite and stars were glittering like jewels flung carelessly across the sky. Nikki was curled up on a sleeping bag and he and Daisy sat across the fire from each other.

While she waited for the water to boil, she reached into her backpack and drew out a couple of large, covered plastic dishes.

"What's that?"

"Dinner!" She grinned at him. "I made more beef pasties late last night to bring along. And I've got some great corn chowder here, too. All we need to do is heat it up."

Surprised again, he shook his head. "You realize this isn't supposed to be a picnic."

"We have to eat and I just thought it would be easier this way. Don't worry," she told him with a tender touch of sarcasm. "Tomorrow we can chew on bark if you insist. But tonight, dinner's on me."

A short laugh shot from his throat. "Chew on bark?"

She tipped her head to one side and looked at him with a bemused expression on her face. "You should do that more often."

"Eat bark?"

"No," she said. *"Smile."*

Jericho watched her then as she expertly scooped coffee into the pot, then sat back to let it boil on the edge of the fire. "You keep surprising me," he said after another moment of shared silence. "I expected you to fold early today."

"I know."

"That why you hung in?"

"Partially, I suppose," she admitted, drawing

her knees up and wrapping both arms around them. "And partially to prove to myself I could do it." She gave him a rueful smile. "I'm not saying my legs aren't screaming at me, or that I'm not so tired I couldn't flop backward over a boulder and fall right asleep, but I did it."

He nodded, willing to give her that much at least. "You did."

"So, does that mean I've proved myself?"

"Not yet," he said, reluctantly thinking about what she had to face on the coming day. She'd be a lot more exhausted tomorrow night than she was at this moment, he thought and realized that he didn't like thinking about that. "You've got to make it through the full two days and nights."

"I will, you know."

Her voice was steel covered in velvet. Soft but strong, and the purpose in her eyes flashed at him in the firelight. "I'm convinced you'll give it a good shot," Jericho said.

"That's something, anyway," she mused.

Just beyond their campsite, the river rushed through the darkness, swiftly moving water sounding like hundreds of sighs rising together. A cold wind swept through the trees and had Daisy tugging the edges of her borrowed coat closer together.

"I can't believe it's so cold up here. In L.A., it's still warm at night."

"We'll probably have first snow by the end of the month."

"Can't wait to see it," she said, her eyes still glittering at him.

"We'll see." Jericho reached out, tapped the coffeepot carefully with his fingertips and, satisfied, picked up a cloth to grab the pot by its curved handle. He poured each of them a cup of the steaming black brew, then watched as Daisy pulled a cook pan closer and dumped her corn chowder into it to heat.

"It'll be ready in a few minutes," she said, picking up her coffee cup for a sip. "So while we wait, tell me about Brant."

That caught him off guard and Jericho's gaze snapped to hers. "What do you mean?"

"I mean, what was it like over there? Was Brant happy where he was—before he died?"

Five

Frowning, Jericho said, "Happy? Nobody's happy on a battlefield."

"You know what I mean," she persisted.

He stared into his coffee as if looking for answers. Finally, he said, "Yeah, I do. The thing is, people always ask that question, but they don't really want to know what a war zone is like."

"I do. I want to know what my brother's life was like before it ended."

Lifting his gaze to hers, he kept his face

deliberately blank. "Brant did his job. He was good at it. He was well-liked."

When she opened her mouth to ask another question, he cut her off. "Daisy, let it go."

"I can't," she told him, regret shining in her whiskey-brown eyes. "I have to know."

Jericho sighed a little, took a drink of his coffee and told her what he could, with some judicious editing. Civilians would never understand what it was like in a combat zone. Would never know the moments of pure adrenaline rush, followed by the searing hours of boredom. They wouldn't understand what it was to put your life in someone else's hands and to trust them with yours, or the fierce loyalty that the military experienced on a daily basis.

And how could they?

So he kept it simple and as vague as he could possibly get away with. "The days were blistering hot and the nights were so cold," he said, "you half expected to wake up with icicles on your nose."

"Brant complained about the cold in an e-mail once. I sent blankets," she told him. "To everyone in his unit."

"I know," he said, giving her a real smile now as his memory raced back in time. "There was a lot of celebrating that day. After that, every mail call, Brant's friends huddled close, wanting to get in on one of your packages from home."

"I'm glad," she said, though her features were wreathed in sadness.

He could give her this much. To let her know that her efforts had been appreciated by more than just her brother. "Touches of home are really cherished when they're hard to come by. I can tell you all of the hot chocolate and instant coffees and dry foods you sent made him real popular. MREs get pretty tasteless after a while."

She nodded. "Meals Ready to Eat. Brant told me about them. He actually had me taste one once. It was tuna casserole." She grimaced.

Jericho laughed. "It's an acquired taste.

Actually, I brought some with me on this trip, just in case. So if you want to—"

"No, thanks," she said, reaching out to give her chowder a stir.

The scent of the soup filled the air and Jericho could admit at least to himself that he was relieved she'd brought along provisions for tonight. What she'd packed looked a hell of a lot better than the MREs.

"You were with him when he died, weren't you?"

The question was so softly asked, posed with such hesitation, the sound of the river nearly drowned it out. But Jericho heard her and also caught the worried expression on her face, as if she were half afraid to hear his answer.

He was stepping onto dangerous ground here. Might as well have been a minefield. Not enough information and she'd still be thirsty for more. Too much information and her dreams would be haunted. No information at all and she'd rag on him until he gave her something.

Again, he kept it simple. "Yeah, I was."

"He wasn't…in pain, was he?"

If he had been, Jericho wouldn't have told her, but as it stood, he could be honest about this at least. "No, he wasn't. He talked about you. Asked me to help you out if you ever needed it."

"My little brother trying to protect me," she mused and looked at him. The trail of a single tear coursed down her cheek like a drop of silver sliding over porcelain.

"That's what brothers do," he said, thinking of his own brothers. Jefferson, Justice and Jesse. He hadn't seen much of them since he'd come home.

By choice, really. He'd wanted, needed, the solitude of the mountain and his brothers had respected that. Of course, he thought with an inward smile, his sisters-in-law were less understanding and had managed to drag him off the mountain for a few family things.

And on those rare occasions, he had been

struck by a surprising jolt of envy that had shamed him some. Hell, he was glad for his brothers. They were all happy, doing what they loved doing—raising families. Jericho had decided as a kid he wasn't interested in living his life in the traditional manner. But seeing his brothers with their families always left him feeling a little like the outsider.

"You have three brothers, don't you?"

"Yeah," he said, jolting from his thoughts.

"Are you close?"

"Used to be," he admitted. "Still are, really, but we grew up, we each chose a different path and we all got busy building lives. Jefferson lives in Ireland now, so no, we don't see much of each other anymore."

"That's a shame," she said, spooning chowder into two bowls and handing him one. "Family is important. It's the *only* important thing."

Which made him remember that now that she'd lost her brother, Daisy had no family.

Though he didn't see much of his, he couldn't really imagine life without them, either.

In the firelight, Daisy looked lovely, delicate, with her soft hair falling over her shoulders, reflections of the flames dancing in her wide, brown eyes. She ate her soup and thought her thoughts and couldn't possibly have known that just looking at her was making him...*want*.

Which just naturally brought to mind Sam's warnings before they'd left the lodge that morning. Maybe the older man was right. Maybe Jericho was just being twitchy and not being fair to her.

But, hell, it was *his* mountain.

Who said he had to be fair?

Jericho watched Daisy maneuver her way carefully across a rope bridge in the early morning light and found himself silently rooting for her. She was a surprise in many ways. Not only did she have spine, she seemed inherently incapable of quitting. She wasn't afraid to try something—take a risk—if it meant getting herself closer to her goal.

Plus her incessant good humor was starting to rub off on him. Hard to maintain a stern demeanor when you were faced down by a brilliant smile every time you turned around. Yeah, she wasn't what he'd expected at all. And though his original opinion that she didn't belong on the mountain still held, he had to give her credit for a hell of a lot more than he would have guessed.

Frowning, he watched her take small steps and then slide her hands along the top rope of the bridge. He'd had several obstacle-course projects made and installed before he'd opened the camp. This was one of his personal favorites.

A single, heavy rope was the base of the bridge with more ropes angling up from the base in a *V*. Stretched between two tall pines, the bridge was only four feet off the ground, so anyone falling wasn't going to die. Though the bruises gathered would be a painful reminder of failure. He'd seen plenty of men topple off that bridge, cursing their own clumsiness and ineptitude, but Daisy was making it. Sure, she was taking twice as long as most people to complete the course, but careful didn't mean failure.

The wind lifted her long ponytail and snapped it like a flag. Her jeans were dirty and her hands were curled so tightly around the guide rail ropes that her knuckles were white. But she was doing it.

He stood below her, watching every step and wanting her to succeed.

"Why does it have to sway so much?" she demanded, not risking a look at him but keeping her gaze fixed, just as he'd told her to, on her final goal.

"It's a *rope*," he reminded her, "bound to sway."

"I don't understand how this is a survival thing," she muttered, scooting her clenched fists farther along the guide ropes. Her feet slid forward another inch or two.

"If you have to get to the other side of a river fast, you'd understand."

"Be faster to swim," she pointed out and gave him a fleeting grin.

"You're doing fine. Pay attention to where you're putting your feet. One in front of the other."

"I know," she said, swallowing hard. "Good thing you made me change out of my boots before we left the lodge. Never would have done this in them."

He smiled to himself and kept pace with her. The dog at the end of the leash he held barked and pranced and in general made a racket as it tried, futilely, to reach Daisy. "How can you concentrate with this dog shooting off its mouth?"

"I'm used to it. Nikki's very chatty," she admitted and one of her feet slipped off the rope. She gasped but caught herself before she could fall. "Whoa, boy. That was close."

"It was." And he didn't want to think about

the feeling that had jolted through him with her misstep. He'd watched dozens, hundreds of people walk this rope bridge and never once before had he had a vested interest in how they managed it.

Lots of them had taken tumbles, too, and it hadn't bothered him a bit. Yet damned if he wanted Daisy falling.

Shaking his head, Jericho acknowledged that he was having a problem. He was supposed to be discouraging her from passing these little tests. Instead, he'd helped her as much as he could. Maybe it was because of her brother, Jericho told himself. Maybe he felt as if he owed her something. But then again, maybe it was just because he wanted her.

He could admit that much to himself. And whatever he was feeling for her had only intensified since that morning. He and Daisy had gone to sleep the night before, lying on opposite sides of the fire.

But the nights were cold at this altitude and

when Jericho woke up this morning, it was to find a curvy, beautiful, warm woman snuggled up close to him, spooning herself along the front of his body. Which completely explained the dream he'd been having, filled with images of hot, sweaty sex. He woke up to an aching groin and his blood pumping fast and thick through his veins. Ever since that moment of wakefulness, his body had been strung taut as a violin string.

"Jericho?"

He snapped out of his thoughts and focused anew. "No more talking. Just concentrate."

"Okay," she countered, keeping her gaze fixed on the end of the rope bridge, "if I can't talk, then you talk to me."

He shook his head. "You're unbelievable."

"That's not talking," she said.

"Fine," he said, tugging on the leash to pull the dog back into line, "I'll talk. Let's see…we've got a batch of clients arriving end of next week. Only be here for a long weekend."

"Who are they?" she asked as her foot slipped. "Whoops!"

"Concentrate."

"Right. I'm good. Fine. Keep talking."

"They're part of a law firm from Indiana," he said. Remembering how the last bunch of lawyers had performed, Jericho wasn't looking forward to it. Lawyers seemed incapable of unwinding. Even in the wilderness, they were wired, tense. Without their PDAs and cell phones, they acted like spoiled children missing a favorite toy. They didn't like being in the outdoors and usually resented being sent here by their companies.

"Not looking forward to it," he said. "Lawyers complain too much."

"True enough. I'm almost across."

She was. Close enough to the end that she was liable to start speeding up to get it over with. "Slow down. Careful steps."

"I am, I am," she told him in an undertone.

"So if you don't like lawyers why have them here?"

"They're paying customers, like anyone else."

"Uh-huh. Did you ever think of opening up the camp to kids?"

"Kids?"

She laughed loud and long, and the joyful sound of it rose up through the trees like smoke. He narrowed his gaze on her and scowled when she set herself swaying wildly with her laughter. "You sound so horrified!"

"Knock it off and pay attention to what you're doing."

"Oh, relax! I'm good. In fact," she added, her voice rising, "I'm *done!*" She stepped onto the platform at the end of the rope bridge and threw both hands into the air in a victory pose. "I did it! By myself!"

Sure, he thought, not counting his shouted instructions and constant watchfulness. But damned if he could deny her the victory dance.

"Yeah, you did. Enough celebrating. Now we go hit the climbing wall."

"Wow, way to pop my balloon."

"You want to be congratulated?" he asked. "Do it all, then we'll talk. Now climb down, take this silly excuse for a dog and let's hike to the wall."

"Climbing a wall?" Her features fell like a kid faced with a pop quiz. That only lasted a second or two, though. She lifted that stubborn chin of hers and said, "Fine. Let's do it."

"Damned if I'm not starting to like you," he said and had the satisfaction of seeing surprise flicker across her face.

"Thanks."

He watched her climb down from the platform and walk toward him with a spring in her step. The little dog on the end of the red leash jumped and pulled, trying to get to her, so Jericho dropped the leash and the poodle raced to Daisy. The tiny dog was scooped up and cuddled while it wiggled in ecstasy.

Jericho thought briefly that he couldn't blame the animal for the reaction. In fact, he almost envied the ridiculous little dog.

"Jericho?"

Her voice sounded confused. "What?"

She smiled at him. "Just wondering where you were. I was talking to you and you just zoned out."

Well, that was humiliating. "I was thinking about the wall," he lied.

"Oh. Okay." She sounded disappointed now, but added, "Let's go and get it over with then."

Get it over with. Hmm. That had been his plan in bringing her up here. Walk her through, watch her fail and get her off the mountain. What the plan was now, he wasn't sure.

"So," she asked as Nikki trotted ahead of them, "why'd you freak when I suggested you bring kids up here?"

"I didn't freak," he said, and assured himself that was true. A man who'd spent as many years in the military as he had wouldn't be "freaked" by the idea of having kids run amok at his camp. "I was just…surprised by the suggestion."

She pushed a low-hanging bough out of her way, ducked her head to pass under and said, "I don't know why. In my old neighborhood, there were dozens of kids who would have loved to be here for a week or two." She took a moment to glance around and he followed her gaze.

Early morning light tipped the edges of the pine branches. A soft wind sighed through the trees and a bright blue jay shot through the air like a colorful bullet. The woods never failed to center him. To give him the sense of peace that was as elusive as it was sought after. Just the thought of having dozens of teenagers rampaging through the forest he considered a sanctuary was enough to make him grit his teeth. But Daisy clearly liked the idea.

"Kids in the city have no idea really. What a world with no sidewalks or freeways looks like," she said wistfully. "They've never seen the stars the way you can up here and I'm sure they've never heard silence so deep."

"I'm not set up to have kids here," he said, guiding her around a stack of boulders. "This is a leadership camp. We train CEOs and other corporate types how to use teamwork. How to count on each other and learn from each other. How to overcome negatives and turn them into positives."

"All of which kids would benefit from learning," she pointed out.

"Not my job," he insisted. What the hell would he do with a dozen or more kids running wild on the mountain? Hell, just the liability issues alone would be staggering.

"You talk tough, but you're not such a hard guy, Jericho King."

One dark eyebrow lifted when he glanced back at her. "Don't kid yourself."

"Oh, I'm not," she said, smiling into his scowling face. "See, I've talked with Kevin, your cook—who is, I hesitate to point out, barely more than a kid himself—"

"He's twenty."

"My point exactly," she said smugly. "Anyway, he told me that not only did you hire him here with no references, but that you're also loaning him the money to go to the Culinary Institute of America. So he can be the chef he dreams of being."

"That's different." And real damn irritating to find out that Kevin was shooting his mouth off. Jericho was going to have to have a talk with the kid.

"How is it different?"

He wasn't sure. Kevin had wandered up to the mountain a little more than a year ago looking for work. He'd been scrawny and exhausted from carrying around a chip on his shoulder for so long. He'd had a rough life but he'd stood up to it and made himself into a good kid despite the odds. He'd proven himself in the kitchen so quickly that Jericho had kept him on. Now, he was helping the kid get a start. No big deal.

Gritting his teeth, he said, "The difference is, I didn't go hunting down a bunch of kids to sponsor. Kevin found us. He just showed up and wouldn't leave. Besides, he stopped being a kid a long time ago. He's been on his own since he was fifteen and—"

"And you gave him a chance to be what he wanted to be," Daisy said, laying one hand on his forearm. "I'm just saying it would be nice if other kids had the same opportunity."

Reluctantly, Jericho pulled free of her touch and said abruptly, "Maybe you should stop worrying about other people and give a thought or two to passing your own test."

That kept her quiet for a while, but in the silence, Jericho's mind raced with the thoughts and ideas she'd planted there.

Damn it.

Six

Daisy was exhausted and every bone and muscle in her body ached like a bad tooth, but beneath the misery was a sense of accomplishment. She'd done it. So far she'd passed his silly tests and was well on her way to earning herself a place at his lodge. He wouldn't be able to send her away now and she was that much closer to having the time to seduce him, make a child and have a family.

Over the past couple of days, she'd gotten to know Jericho King better than she would have

by dating him for a month. Even though he re-
sisted conversation, she'd been able to pry words
out of him. And she'd had the opportunity to
watch him. To study him. There was a sense
of quiet confidence about him that was very
attractive, and she had to admit that his stoic
standoffishness only added to it.

There was a closeness between them now that
under normal circumstances would never have
happened so quickly. They'd worked together to
make camp, to eat, to live. They'd slept curled
up together...well, she thought, they had as soon
as she'd moved over to him for warmth and
stayed to snuggle. They'd talked more than most
couples did in a week and they'd each learned
something about the other, she told herself. He
had learned that she wasn't going to quit and go
away.

And she had learned that he was unlike any
other man she'd ever known. He seemed so solitary. So comfortable with his aloneness that
Daisy was drawn closer and closer in an attempt

to breach the walls he'd erected around himself so completely.

"These plants are edible," he was saying, "if you dig them up and pound the root. Won't be tasty, but it would keep you alive."

She nodded as if she were making mental notes, but she didn't care about edible roots. After all, she wouldn't be wandering the forest foraging for food. Once her test was finished, she'd be at the lodge and wouldn't step into the woods again without an experienced guide.

So instead, she watched the man. Jericho moved through the trees with a confidence born of self-reliance. He was a complex man. He hadn't wanted her here and hadn't made that a secret. But earlier, when he could have stood back and watched her struggle to climb the stupid wall—watched her fail—he hadn't. Instead, he'd planted one big hand under her behind and boosted her up enough that Daisy was able to scramble to the top and then drop over the other side, victorious.

She knew she never would have been able to make that climb under her own steam. Hard to admit, but she simply didn't have the upper-body strength to accomplish the task.

"Your best bet, if you're lost in the woods, is to stay put," Jericho told her, glancing over his shoulder at her to make sure she was paying attention.

"Hug a tree. Right."

He shook his head and sighed. "But you wouldn't stay in one place, would you?"

"Probably not," she agreed cheerfully.

"Fine, so at least figure a way to mark your trail, so those looking for you can find you."

"Good idea." She gave him a wide smile and nodded as he showed her how to snap the ends of branches, or lay out rocks in an arrow pattern or— *Oh,* she thought, *let's face it.* If she was lost up here, she'd probably die. So she just wouldn't get lost.

"Wouldn't it be easier if I never left the lodge?" she asked.

"Yeah," he said, straightening up to look down at her. "But you will. It's in your nature. At least tell someone where you're going when you do."

"I can do that." She smiled again. "You realize that you just admitted that I'm staying on?"

"I'm considering it. You passed that test," he grudgingly admitted. "Though you still have to make the campfire yourself tonight and cook dinner you didn't bring with you, not to mention making it back to the lodge alive."

"I will."

He ignored that. "We'll find dinner, then the responsibility's on you."

"I can do it," she said firmly. "You'll see."

He shook his head and sighed a little.

"So," she asked, "what's next, *boss?*"

"We're headed home. We'll camp by the river again tonight on our way back."

"Let's go, Nikki," she called out and the little dog raced back to her, ears flapping, tiny feet flying across the pine needle–littered forest

floor. Nikki paused in passing Jericho long
enough to snarl at him, then leaped into Daisy's
waiting arms.

He muttered something she thought it was just
as well she hadn't quite heard. Then she asked,
"So why did you help me? You could have let
me fail, but you didn't."

He shrugged. "You would have made it. Eventually."

"No, I wouldn't," she admitted, though it cost
her. "I was beat and just hanging by my fingertips when you gave me that boost. So why?"

He stopped, looked back at her and with his
features set in an unreadable mask, said simply,
"I respect guts. And you've got 'em."

When he turned around to continue leading
the way to the river, Daisy inhaled sharply and
felt a swell of pride rise up and burst inside
her. It was a compliment casually given from a
man who wasn't used to giving them at all. She
couldn't have felt more proud and satisfied if
he'd handed her a medal.

* * *

"You're going to kill the bunny?"

Jericho heard the outraged tremor in Daisy's voice and knew that he wouldn't be eating rabbit stew for supper. He'd set the snare early that morning when they broke camp, knowing they'd be camping here again tonight. And he'd been pleased to find a nice fat rabbit waiting to be dinner. He should have known it wouldn't be that easy.

He looked up into her wide, distressed eyes. "It was going to be dinner," he said.

"Oh, my God." She looked at him as if he were some mad dog serial killer. "I can't eat a bunny."

"Yeah. I'm getting that." The trapped rabbit scampered in place, desperately trying to get free of the rope that had tightened around one of its hind feet. Jericho looked at it and sighed. Then he bent down, loosened the rope and straightened up as the rabbit scooted off into the underbrush. Dry pine straw rustled under the animal's running feet and then there was silence, the only sound the rushing of the nearby river.

"I can't believe you did that," Daisy said as Jericho turned to face her.

He shrugged off her gratitude. "You weren't going to eat it so…"

"Thank you." She said it simply and honestly and Jericho nodded.

"You're welcome. Now, I'm going to go catch some trout for dinner—" He took a step, stopped and looked at her again. "Unless you've got a soft spot for fish, too."

"Nope. Pan-fried, baked, grilled, barbecued, even smooshed in a blender to make a mousse," she assured him. "I like it all."

"Good to know," he told her, shaking his head, "though here's something to keep in mind if you do end up with this job…"

"Yes?"

"I don't eat fish mousse."

"I'll make a note," she said, one corner of her mouth lifting into a half smile.

"Good." He turned around again, headed for the river, when Daisy stopped him by calling his name. "Yeah?"

She came to him in three long strides, wrapped her arms around his waist and gave him a hard hug. "Thank you. For the rabbit."

She was so close, so warm, pressed so intimately against him that all of Jericho's carefully designed reticence and resistance melted away. He'd been on edge for the past two days. Damn hard to maintain a tough shell around a woman so determinedly positive. But he'd cautioned himself to keep that safe distance between them. To not get drawn in by big amber eyes and a wide, welcoming smile.

But she was the kind of woman who got under a man's skin whether he wanted her there or not. Hell, he'd been fighting the urge to kiss her for hours. No, that urge had been with him since the moment she'd first stepped out of her car to sprawl across his lawn.

Now, with her lush curves leaning into him and her full, delectable mouth curved into a smile directed at him, how was he supposed to resist temptation? He doubted any red-blooded male would have been able to.

So he did what his body demanded and silently told his mind to butt out. Cupping her face in his palms, he held her still and watched as her eyes widened, softened, then slowly slid closed. A soft sigh of anticipation slipped from between her lips and Jericho kissed her.

The first taste of her was electric—incredible—and only fueled his hunger for more. He deepened the kiss and felt her surrender. Felt his own body begin a slow burn that enveloped him from head to toe. He held her face and moved his mouth over hers, parting her lips with his tongue, sliding into her mouth to capture the essence of her and draw it into himself.

His body tightened until he thought he might

just explode from the agony of want. She moaned softly and he echoed that small sound and felt it build within him. Seconds ticked past, became minutes and might have spun into hours and he wouldn't have known. Wouldn't have sensed anything beyond the sensations roaring through him.

And that random thought was enough to bring him up and out of those feelings like a drowning man breaching the surface of a lake. He came up gasping, his heartbeat thundering in his chest, his blood pounding in his ears. He'd lost himself in her. Completely lost control in a way that hadn't happened to him in years. He didn't like it.

She opened her eyes and looked directly into his. Her mouth was soft and lush and he wanted nothing more than to taste her again. To lay her down on the forest floor and bury himself deep inside her. And because that craving was so strong, he took a single, deliberate step back. What the hell was he doing?

If he had any sense left at all, he'd get her off his mountain so damn fast, she'd be nothing but a blur of motion. But could he *not* give her the job because he didn't trust himself around her?

If he hired her, she'd be a constant source of temptation. If he didn't, wouldn't it be as if he'd sent her away for his own peace of mind? And wouldn't that make him a damn coward? He'd promised Brant Saxon to help his sister if she needed it.

He owed that kid, too, Jericho told himself and briefly recalled the eager young man who'd died too soon. The guilt still haunted him. Regret a constant companion. Was Jericho really going to turn his back on a promise made to a dying comrade? Daisy Saxon was here. Now. She needed the help he'd once promised to give.

And if he turned her away, it would be not because she'd failed, not because she didn't belong, but because Jericho King had encountered a woman who worried him.

Pushing those and other even more disturbing thoughts out of his mind, Jericho said, "Okay, that didn't just happen."

"It didn't?" She blinked at him and her eyes looked dazed.

He knew the feeling, but damned if he'd admit it. "No, it didn't. I'm the boss, you're the cook and that's where it all ends." He backed up again and half turned toward the river. He took a step, stopped and said over his shoulder, "Start the campfire. I'll go catch some fish for dinner."

As he walked away, Daisy lifted her fingers to her lips, enjoying the buzz of sensation lingering there and whispered, "Shouldn't be a problem starting the fire. I'm already going up in flames."

As they finished eating two hours later, stars swept across an indigo sky. He hadn't said much, Daisy mused. But then, he hadn't had to. She'd known exactly what he was thinking without him saying a word. Mostly because she was

thinking the same thing. That kiss they'd shared
had set off a chain reaction inside her that was
still fizzing like a lit sparkler.

She'd come to him wanting a child. Now, she
also wanted *him*. Which complicated the situation, but didn't really change anything. And
oddly enough, the more he withdrew, the more
she was drawn to him. What did that say about
her?

When she gathered up the dishes and the pan
she'd used to cook in and stacked them to carry
to the river to wash, Jericho beat her to it. "I'm
supposed to be doing all of this, remember?" she
said. "Part of the whole survival-prove-you're-
worthy test?"

He smirked at her, shook his head and carried the small load to the river. She fell into
step behind him, determined to earn her way.
She'd cooked a good dinner. At least, she was
taking the fact that Jericho had eaten two of the
fish himself as a good sign. But part of being

outdoors, camping, was the cleanup and she wouldn't walk away from a job half done.

"Seriously, I'm cleaning up." She caught him at the river, took the plates and pan from him and dropped to her knees in the sand beside the rushing water. He crouched, too, and waited until she met his gaze to speak again.

"Accepting help doesn't mean you can't do it yourself."

"I know, but you're the one who said it was all up to me and I want to do this. I want to prove to you that I can do this job."

"You already have."

That stopped her. "Really?"

He shrugged, glanced away, then looked back at her and gave her a reluctant smile. "You're a good campfire cook."

"Yeah?" Ridiculously pleased, Daisy grinned. "Thanks, I did notice you ate a lot."

He laughed shortly. "Yeah, well, I've never had pan-fried trout with an herb sauce on the trail."

"Well, I brought along a few things from the lodge kitchen. With the right spices, you can make any meal a banquet..."

"So I'm learning."

It only took a few minutes to clean up the dishes and then they were walking back to the campfire, a companionable silence stretching out between them. Once the supplies had been put away, she sat down across from him. And the quiet lingered, becoming a tension that felt almost brittle. Daisy spoke up finally, because she never had been able to be quiet for long anyway.

Besides, it was time to find out exactly where she stood. She took a breath and faced the hard truth. She wanted to bring up the subject before he did, so that she could put her own spin on her less-than-stellar performance on his series of "tests."

He'd admitted that he was considering giving her the job, and if his decision was going to be based on her skills at his tests, then she wanted to defend herself before he made his final decision.

"About the rope bridge," she began. "I know I didn't go very fast, but I did eventually make it."

"You did."

"And I think if I'd had a little more time—" *like a million years,* she added silently "—I probably could have made it over the climbing wall on my own steam."

"You did better than some I've seen."

That was a bit lowering, she thought. Not good, she told herself, but better than some. Remembering just how poorly she'd done at the climbing, she could only feel sorry for whoever was actually worse than her.

"All in all, you did a good job," Jericho said and Daisy's thoughtful gaze narrowed on him. He shrugged. "Frankly, I didn't expect you to hold up as well as you have."

"Oooh. Big surprise." She smiled though, giving him silent encouragement to keep talking. If he was feeling generous toward her, she wanted to hear it.

"Right. Well." Firelight danced across his features, tossing shadow and light over the sharp planes of his face, making his guarded eyes even more difficult to read than they normally were. "Like I said, you've got spine. And that's important. Maybe more important than being able to climb a wall on your own."

"So I didn't lose points because you had to give me a boost?"

"No," he said. "You didn't ask for help, after all."

"True," she said eagerly. "And I wouldn't have."

"I know."

"So you said earlier, you were considering giving me the job." Daisy took another deep breath and blurted out her question. "Have you decided? Because if your mind still isn't made up, we can go back to the wall. I can try it again. I'm pretty sure I could do it with enough time…"

He chuckled briefly. "You really don't know the meaning of quit, do you?"

"Not when I really want something," she admitted.

"Yeah, I get that. So we don't have to go back to the wall."

"You've made your decision, then."

"I have." He nodded. "If you still want the job, you have it."

"Really?" Bubbles of excitement burst into life inside her. Funny, but she hadn't realized just how stressed she'd been about this. If he hadn't offered her the job, she'd had no backup plan. No way to convince him to let her stay. No strategy for getting him into bed and making her pregnant. Now, thankfully, one wouldn't be needed. She'd be here, on the mountain with him, every day.

Every night.

And soon, she'd have the baby, the family

she wanted so badly. All she had to do was say yes.

"Of course I want the job," she told him.

"All right then, it's settled."

But he didn't look happy about it. "Can I ask you something?"

"Why not?"

"Why are you being nice to me?" Maybe she shouldn't push her luck. Maybe she should just accept his job offer at face value and count her blessings. But Daisy had to know why he'd decided in her favor. "We both know I never would have passed your tests if you hadn't helped me. So why did you?"

He scrubbed one hand across his face and blew out a breath. Then he shifted his gaze to the flames dancing in the fire ring to avoid looking directly at her. "I came out here expecting you to fail, like I said."

To be honest, so had she. "And…"

"And you didn't." He looked directly into her eyes. "You didn't quit. Didn't whine. Didn't give in. You kept pushing yourself no matter what."

Daisy smiled. "So blind stubbornness earns points with you?"

One corner of his mouth lifted briefly. "You could say that."

"Well, yay me."

"We'll see."

"About what?"

"How you'll work out around here. Yes, you're hired, but that's not saying you're going to want to stay."

"I won't quit." Not until she had what she'd come here for. Not until she was pregnant. Her gaze drifted to his mouth, his firm, soft lips and everything inside her tingled, as if her whole body had been asleep and was suddenly waking up. Then he started talking again and those tingles subsided just a bit.

"Like I said, I like your attitude. But know this. Stubborn might not be enough to keep you here when the snow starts flying and you're

cut off from the main road for days at a time."
He laid his forearm across one updrawn knee
and looked at her across the fire. "It's not easy
living up here. You're a woman not used to the
quiet—"

"I like the quiet," she argued.

He laughed shortly. "You can't be quiet yourself for more than ten minutes at a stretch."

She frowned, but could hardly disagree.

"I'm just saying, if you figure out this isn't
what you want after all, there's no shame in
walking away."

Daisy tipped her head to one side and watched
him. "And you expect me to, is that it?"

"I didn't say that."

"You didn't have to," she told him. "Still, I
guess the only way to convince you that I'm right
for this job is to prove it to you. Yet again."

He nodded. "You're getting your chance."

"That's all I ever asked for." Daisy knew he
still didn't believe that she could make it there,
but she'd show him. She'd convince him. And

then, she thought, remembering that simmering kiss, she would seduce him.

She had to admit that she was looking forward to the coming seduction with a lot more eagerness now than she had when she first arrived. There were dark fires simmering inside Jericho King. She'd felt the heat of them all too briefly and couldn't wait for the chance to experience it again. And when they did, he wouldn't be telling her that it hadn't happened. Smiling to herself, she gasped when the first, eerie howl lifted into the air.

"What was that?"

"Coyote."

"Oh, God." She blew out a breath and pretended to not be shaken by the wild, eerie sound still reverberating through the mountains. "I didn't hear them last night."

"Probably farther away then. They move around a lot, but they always come back to their home ground."

"Which is here," she mused, staring off into the darkened forest surrounding them.

"They were here first," he told her with a shrug.

"Well, that makes me feel so much better." She'd get used to it, she told herself firmly. After all, it wasn't as if she had to *live* outside with wild animals. She and Nikki would have their own room at the main lodge and they'd be careful to not stray too far from the... *Nikki*.

Daisy turned her head, looking for her dog and felt her heart chill when she didn't see the tiny poodle. Now that she thought of it, she hadn't seen Nikki since dinner. As if to deliberately terrify her, another howl from what was probably a very hungry coyote lifted into the air.

Seven

"Jericho," she cried, "Nikki's gone. Nikki! Nikki baby, come to Mommy."

She jumped to her feet as yet one more howl sounded out, sending shivers down her spine. That one seemed closer than the one before, she thought frantically. How many of the blasted things were out there?

"Damn dog," Jericho muttered, scrambling to his feet as Daisy began to walk a fast, frenetic circle around the fire. She peered into the woods, struggling to see past the encroaching dark, straining to hear the slightest sound, the faintest yip. But there was nothing. It was as if the forest had swallowed up her dog.

"Where is she?" Daisy sent a quick, panicked look at Jericho. "She must have wandered off when I wasn't looking. Oh, God, how could I have been so careless? Nikki!"

Before he could say anything, Daisy rushed off blindly into the tree line, pushed by a driving sense of urgency. If there were coyotes close by, Nikki would be helpless. Nothing more than a snack to an animal three times her size.

With her heart in her throat, Daisy shoved through low-hanging pine branches, hardly noticing when the limbs and needles poked at her. "Nikki! Come here, girl!"

"Daisy, damn it!" His shout followed her into the brush but didn't stop her.

Her gaze swept the darkness, checking every shadow. Beside herself with worry now, she called the dog to her again and then listened for an answering bark that never came. The farther she got from the river, the more terrified she became. Nikki wouldn't have strayed this far. But she might have gone another way. How would Daisy find her? They should go to the lodge. Get a search party. Flashlights. Something. But she couldn't leave without Nikki, so Jericho would have to go for help alone.

She'd wait here. She'd keep looking. She had to find the little dog that was her last remaining link to the brother she'd lost. Visions of Nikki hurt, or worse, filled her mind and strangled the breath in her lungs. Her imagination was running at full steam so she screamed when a hand came down on her arm and spun her around.

"Stop," he ground out, holding onto her upper arms. "You're not going to find the damn dog running through the woods like a crazy woman. Hell, you don't even know where you are. How can you find her if you're lost, too?"

"I'll find her. I'll just keep looking until I do. I can't lose her," she said, her voice hardly more than a whisper. "She's all I have. She's my family. She's..."

He gave her a hard shake to get her attention, then released her and stepped back. "You go running off like that in the dark and you're going to end up at the bottom of a ravine. You don't know these woods."

"No, but you do," Daisy said, grabbing hold of his shirt with both hands. "Find her, Jericho. Please find her."

Clearly disgusted, he said, "I'm going to. But you're going back to camp." He turned her around, pointed her at their campsite and gave her a gentle shove. "Go back now and wait by the fire or I'll be looking for you *and* the stupid dog."

She wanted to argue. Wanted to tell him that she wouldn't be sent off to wait for the big strong man to come to her rescue. But even as she started to speak, Daisy realized he was right. She'd only slow him down. He knew these woods. This was his territory and she'd only make his search that much more difficult if she insisted on going along.

So for Nikki's sake, she'd do what he said. She'd sit down and she'd wait. "Okay. Okay, I will. But find her, Jericho. She must be so scared…"

Muttering darkly under his breath, he jerked his head at her, silently telling her to go back. Then he moved off without so much as a whisper of sound and disappeared into the deep shadows of the forest.

Daisy shivered and walked back to the campsite. She waited, but she couldn't sit. How could she? She was alone by a campfire, and Jericho was off moving through the darkness in silence and Nikki… If anything happened to her dog…

Daisy continued to pace in tight, worried circles around the perimeter of the campfire, her mind racing, her heart pounding. The coyotes howled again and she wondered if they were hungry. If they'd already spotted a tiny poodle snack. If Jericho would never find the little dog because she'd already been…

"She's fine." Jericho's voice broke into Daisy's thoughts and she whirled around to face him.

He stepped into the firelight and held a trembling Nikki against his chest in one huge hand.

"You found her!" Daisy raced to him, scooped up her dog, murmuring soothing sounds and sighs as Jericho watched her with a bemused expression on his face. "Where was she?"

Nikki's tiny pink tongue swiped Daisy's face in gratitude just before the little dog sent Jericho a look of complete canine adoration.

"Cowering under a rock," he said, with a shake of his head. "She was shaking so hard, the leaves on the bush beside her were trembling. Quite the ferocious little watchdog you've got there."

"You're making fun of her, but you saved her. Poor baby, alone in the woods." She looked at him, her heart in her eyes and felt something inside her tremble as violently as Nikki was. "Thank you for finding her. I was so scared."

"It's fine. She's fine."

"I don't know what I would have done if anything had happened to her."

"Nothing did."

"Because of you. My hero."

He stopped, frowned and told her succinctly, "I'm nobody's hero."

But he was, Daisy thought as she watched him walk down to the river, effectively closing himself off. Jericho King might be a reluctant hero, Daisy told herself, but that didn't change the facts. He was a man to count on. A man to admire.

The perfect man to be the father of her child.

He woke up with both Daisy and the dog curled up into him again and this time, it was even more difficult to ignore the warmth of her curvy body pressed up against his. Now he knew what she tasted like. Now he knew what it was like to hold her, to feel her surrender herself. And now he was being haunted by those memories. Which only made him more determined to ignore the feelings, the temptations racing through him.

She was now officially his employee and he wouldn't take advantage of the situation. A man had to have rules of conduct for himself, or he was nothing. Besides, he wasn't the kind of man to allow a woman into his life and Daisy was in no way the one-night-stand kind of female. She had "commitment" stamped all over her. All he had to do was look into her eyes and he could practically see a white picket fence and 2.5 kids—not to mention her idiot dog.

Jericho eased away from her, despite the reluctance nagging at him. He wasn't going to step into a bear trap and he wasn't going to indulge himself and hurt her. So he'd just keep his distance whatever it took and hope that she got over this whim of hers to live on the mountain.

"Daisy!" His voice was sharper than it should have been, but even as he thought that, he figured it was just as well. He didn't want her getting attached to him because nothing good would come of it.

"Huh? What?" She rolled over, the dog yipped and shot up to all four feet while Daisy was still blinking sleep out of her eyes. "What's going on? It's *dark*."

"Almost dawn," he corrected, giving one quick look at the already-lightening sky. "Time to get moving."

"Right," she said, nodding as she pushed herself into a sitting position. "I'll fix breakfast and then we can—"

"We're going now," he told her. No more cozy meals, just the two of them over a dancing fire. "There's trail mix in my pack. You can eat on the way."

"Ooh, yummy," she murmured dryly, scrubbing both hands over her face. "Why the hurry?"

He looked down at her. Eyes slumberous, hair tangled and falling about her face, lips full and all too tempting. *She* was the damn hurry, he thought angrily. Being alone with her was turning into a lesson in torture. One he, thankfully, didn't have to put up with. He'd just get her back to the lodge, let her settle in and from now on, he'd make sure he was never alone with her. Safer all the way around.

His body didn't agree, but it would just have to find a way to deal with disappointment.

"Test is over," he said shortly, going down on one knee to stuff supplies into his pack. "Time to get back to work."

"Okay…" She pushed to her feet and Nikki trotted to Jericho's side, sat beside him and leaned against his thigh. "I'll just…"

He paused in his packing, shot her a look and nodded. "Fine. Go take care of things, but hurry it up."

While Daisy stepped into the forest for some privacy, Jericho looked down at the little dog snuggling in close to him. "You and your mistress are turning out to be a real pain in the ass." When the dog only huffed out a contented sigh, Jericho scowled at it. "You're not going to get to me though, either of you."

"Anyone want seconds?" Daisy asked, lifting the cast-iron skillet temptingly.

Firelight danced across her features, highlighting her grin and making her look more beautiful than Jericho had ever seen her.

"Count me in," Max Stuben, CEO of a furniture dynasty, spoke up, holding his plate out. "Daisy, after seeing what you can do over a campfire, I have half a mind to go home and shoot my chef."

She laughed, delighted, then said, "A little extreme, Max, but I appreciate the compliment. Jericho and I like to keep our clients happy, don't we?"

When she looked up at him, Jericho couldn't

help smiling back. Damned if the woman hadn't charmed every one of his clients.

Harry Morrison, bank president, added, "I'm impressed with how well you handle yourself out on the trail, Daisy. Why, if my wife were here, she'd be complaining about everything. You seem to love it."

Jericho slid a glance to watch her reaction. She was the least likely woman ever to enjoy being on the mountain, yet she seemed to be doing just that.

"Well, at King Adventure, we really go out of our way to make sure all of our employees are capable of doing everything we ask of our clients. Isn't that right, Jericho?" She looked over at him, a wide smile still on her face.

"That's right," he said, remembering her own tests and how determined she had been to win.

"And maybe," Daisy said to Harry, "your wife wouldn't complain as much if she felt more support."

Chagrined, Harry just shrugged off the comment and Jericho had to hand it to her. She'd very nicely defended a woman she'd never met.

"When you're finished there, we'll clean up and sack out," Jericho said. "We'll be getting an early start in the morning."

"Slave driver," Max muttered good-naturedly.

"You have no idea," Daisy said with a laugh. Then she picked up a few things and carried them down to the water's edge.

Jericho followed after her and when he stopped by her side, she said, "I think it's going well, don't you?"

"Yeah, it is. How are you doing?"

"Great!" When he just looked at her, though, she shrugged and said, "Okay, I admit, I don't love the trail as much as you do, but I can do this."

"You don't have to, you know. You can work at the lodge without making these trips."

She scrubbed at one of the plates and when it was clean to her satisfaction, she set it on a towel and picked up the next one. "I want to show you that I can do this."

"You don't have anything left to prove, Daisy."

"Maybe," she said, "but it's important to me to carry my own weight."

"You treat these guys any better and they're going to be trying to hire you away."

She laughed a little. "Max already offered to back me in opening my own restaurant. But I think he was kidding."

Frowning, Jericho glanced back at the men sitting beside the fire. "I'm not so sure."

Daisy stood up and laid one hand on his forearm. "No worries, Jericho. I'm exactly where I want to be."

She picked up the clean dishes and walked toward camp, leaving Jericho staring after her. The problem here was, Daisy was exactly where he wanted to be, too.

Only two weeks had passed, and Jericho was a man possessed. He spent most days doing everything he could to avoid being around Daisy. But it seemed that no matter what, she found a way to be near him. Her scent clung to the air of the main house. Every breath he drew reminded him of her.

Her laughter rang out and his ears were attuned for the sound, even from rooms away. The meals she prepared were raved about and even their clients, the fussy lawyers and busy bureaucrats, were charmed by her.

He couldn't even escape her at night. His dreams were full of her. And the knowledge that her room was only three doors down the hall from his plagued his mind constantly.

Her dog wasn't helping the situation any, either. Ever since he'd found the little thing that last night in the forest, the poodle had officially adopted him. He could hardly take a step without watching first where he set his boot, afraid he'd crush the damn thing. He'd taken plenty of ribbing about his newfound friend from the other guys, too. Hell, he'd often thought about getting a dog himself, but his plans hadn't included a dog so small it could sit on the palm of his hand.

"Is there a reason you look like you want to bite through a brick?"

Jericho came up out of his dark thoughts with a fierce scowl on his face. He turned on his old friend and said, "This is all your fault, you know."

"What'd I do?" Sam argued, his own features twisting up into a frown.

"You brought Daisy here. You're the one who offered her the damn job." Of course *Jericho* was the one who had hired her, but that was beside the point. "She doesn't belong and she never will and pretending otherwise is just making a bad situation worse."

Sam's features cleared up and a smile tugged at his mouth. "She's getting to you, isn't she?"

"Hell, no, she's not," he lied. Damned if he'd admit to Sam what he couldn't admit to himself. "She's just a distraction is all."

"She is that," Sam agreed and opened a stall door to pour feed for one of the horses. When he was finished, he stepped back, closed the stall again and walked to the next one. "A pretty woman's always a distraction. And one that can cook, too?" He whistled, low and long, shaking his head for emphasis. "Well, that woman's a treasure to a man who isn't too stupid to see what's right in front of him."

Jericho stared at his friend's back hard enough to bore holes right through his body. "Now I'm stupid?"

"Didn't say that, but won't argue the point, you being the boss and all."

"Thanks very much," Jericho muttered and shot a look toward the main house. The barn doors were open, watery winter sunlight slanting across the neatly swept stone floor. Inside the house, Daisy would be bustling around the kitchen preparing lunch for the employees. She was probably singing, he told himself, in that slightly off-key voice of hers. His insides stirred at the thought, and he told himself he was in bad shape.

"You're the one making yourself miserable, you know," Sam told him casually as he continued making his rounds down the row of horse stalls. "Nobody else here has a problem with her. She's doing a good job and she's nice on top of it."

"Nice."

Sam shot him a look. "Yeah, nice. You might want to try it."

Oh, that was the problem, Jericho thought, shoving both hands into his jeans pockets. He wanted to be *more* than nice to her. He wanted her under him, over him. He wanted to slide his hands over those luscious curves, look down into her whiskey eyes and see his own desire-ravaged face reflected back at him. And he wanted it now.

"You don't know what you're talking about," he muttered and stalked out of the barn. What he needed, he told himself, was a hard hike up the mountain. Maybe a night or two on his own. Get his mind clear. Get his sense of control and order back. Get the hell away from Daisy Saxon before she drove him completely crazy.

Daisy was worried.

Jericho had been gone for two nights already and, with no signs of coming back, he was about to make it three. He'd disappeared up the mountain with hardly more than a word to her or anyone else. Sam didn't know where he'd gone—or he simply wasn't saying—and the other guys were just as clueless.

They didn't seem concerned either. They only said that Jericho did this from time to time and she shouldn't worry herself over it. But how could she not?

She'd become accustomed to seeing him every day. To hearing him move around the house. To knowing that he was right down the hall from her every night. Without him there, something vital was missing. Even Nikki was moping around the house as if she'd lost her best friend.

The house was closed up for the night. There were no clients at the moment and the other employees lived in a separate log home on the other side of the compound. She and Nikki were alone and though she wasn't scared, she was uneasy. Wrapping her arms around her middle, she shivered in her short cotton nightgown and stared out her bedroom window at the moonlit darkness beyond the glass.

"Where are you?" she murmured.

How long was he going to stay out there on his own? Why was he gone? She'd so hoped they'd made a connection on their two days in the woods together. She remembered with perfect clarity that deep, lingering kiss that still had her waking up in the middle of the night with her body aching and her heartbeat racing.

How could he just leave? Doesn't he care if people worry?

Behind her on the bed, Nikki whined in sympathy.

But Daisy didn't want sympathy. She wanted Jericho. Home. Where he belonged. Funny, but she hadn't even realized until this moment that she'd already begun to think of this place as home. Strange how quickly she'd acclimated to being here. To this way of life. So completely different from life in the city, living on the mountain was slower yet so much more…fundamental. Here, everyone worked together to make sure life moved as it should. The employees at the camp were a family and she'd slid into their company so easily, she'd come to rely on all of them.

But when the head of their family was missing…

"Darn it, where *are* you?"

Chewing at her bottom lip, she ignored the growing chill in the room and wondered what it would be like here when the snow came. Would she still be here? Would Jericho still be avoiding her? Or would she be pregnant and already gone from this place?

The thought of that sent a curl of regret unspooling at the pit of her stomach. She'd never planned to stay here forever. But now that she'd been here a while, become a part of things, the thought of leaving left her feeling...empty.

But she would have her child, she reminded herself. She wouldn't be alone anymore.

She would have her own family again.

"If he ever comes back," she muttered.

Behind her, Nikki suddenly jumped onto all fours and let out a yip of excitement. Daisy turned to look at her dog, then swung around to gaze out the window again. Jericho, bathed in moonlight, stepped from the tree line and walked across the wide yard, stopping directly in front of the house.

Nikki leaped off the bed, hit the wood floor and skidded, her short nails clacking against the oak planks as she raced for the closed bedroom door.

But Daisy wasn't watching her dog. Instead, her gaze was locked on the man standing in the yard. Moonlight stretched his shadow across the grass and outlined him in a pearly light that seemed otherworldly. In the stillness, he tipped his head back, looked up at her window and met her gaze. Heat sizzled through her and a part of her was amazed that she could feel such an intense reaction from the man at such a distance. She lifted one hand and laid her palm against the cold windowpane as if she could touch him if she concentrated hard enough. And in that instant, something of her thoughts must have transmitted themselves to him because his features went hard and taut and a moment later, he was stalking toward the house with purposeful strides.

Daisy whirled around, grabbed up her robe from the end of her bed and pulled it on as she raced across the room. She threw the door open and Nikki burst free, flying down the hall and then the stairs, headed for the front door. The little dog got there just as Jericho opened it and when he stopped on the threshold, Nikki went up on her hind legs and waved her forepaws at him in celebration.

Daisy stood at the top of the stairs, breath caught in her chest as she watched him bend down, scoop up the dog and stoically accept Nikki's kisses.

"She missed me," he said, his voice low and rough.

"She's not the only one," Daisy told him. Her earlier frustrations and worry and anger were forgotten now in the rush of heat swimming through her system. Just looking at him made her knees weak. Locking her gaze with his fed her fantasies and sent her pulse rate into a gallop.

His mouth went straight and grim. He set the dog on the floor then closed the front door behind him.

"Why did you leave?"

"To get some distance from you." His eyes

were stormy, dark, and flashed with emotions that shifted too quickly for her to make sense of them.

"How's that working for you?"

One corner of his amazing mouth lifted briefly. "Not well."

"I'm glad."

"You shouldn't be," he said and dropped his pack beside the door. Shrugging out of his jacket, he tossed it at the hall tree and didn't seem to care when it missed and fell to the floor.

Daisy's insides twisted as she drew one long, shaky breath. She hadn't expected this, she thought wildly. Hadn't thought that he would be the one to come to her. She'd expected to have to seduce him into bed. But looking into his eyes left her little doubt that Jericho King was a man on a mission.

And lucky her, *she* was that mission. She felt it. She sensed it in the very air surrounding them. It was bristling with tension, with a sexual energy and heat that was strong enough to light a dozen homes through a cold, dark winter.

She laid one hand on the banister and held on as she watched him walk slowly toward the staircase.

"I knew you were going to be trouble," he said tightly. "The minute I saw you, I knew."

"Is that right?"

"Tried to get rid of you, remember? Tried to talk you out of staying."

"You did," she agreed.

"But when you wouldn't listen, I decided to just ignore you," he admitted, taking the steps with a deliberate slowness. "Finally went out on the mountain just to get some space. Clear my head. Thought I could put you out of my mind, but you wouldn't go. You stayed."

Heat pooled in her belly then dipped lower, warming her through and setting up a tingling ache that throbbed at her center.

"I think about you even when I know I shouldn't," he told her as he came closer.

"I've been thinking about you, too," she told him and her heartbeat fluttered unsteadily. "And you were gone so long, I was worried about you."

He snorted. "You should be worried about *you*."

"You don't scare me." She lifted her chin and tossed her hair back from her face. The fire in his eyes glinted at her as he moved steadily closer. Daisy took a breath and held it, not sure she'd be able to draw another. He was big and powerful and looked just a little dangerous and, oh, her entire being was quaking with banked eagerness.

When he stopped on the step just below her, their eyes were level and he said softly, "I should, Daisy. I should scare the hell outta you."

She studied him for a long moment and saw past the desire and the heat in his eyes to the shadows lurking deep within. Shaking her head, she reached out to cup his cheek in her palm and whispered, "You're no danger to me, Jericho King."

He covered her hand with his own. "No," he agreed, "but I can't say the same for your virtue."

Daisy laughed, but the sound was cut off as Jericho grabbed her and slammed her close to his chest. Her head fell back and her eyes were linked with his when she nodded slowly, telling him silently that she wanted him as badly as he did her. Then she said, "My virtue isn't an issue. My need for you is."

"Thank God," he muttered and tossed her over one shoulder.

She yelped in surprise, but Jericho paid no attention. He'd damn near killed himself getting back to the lodge while the moon was still high. He'd wanted her to himself. He'd finally accepted that he wasn't going to get any peace until he'd satisfied his body inside hers. And tonight was the night. He slipped one hand beneath her nightgown and caressed her panty-covered behind as he hit the landing and started down the hall for his room.

"No more waiting," he told her. "No more thinking and dreaming about this. Tonight, I'm going to make you scream my name until you're hoarse."

She shivered and a tiny moan escaped her throat. His own body tightened at the images racing through his mind and he hurried his steps. The little dog nipped along at his heels, but he couldn't have cared less. He reached his bedroom, walked across the wide space and tossed Daisy onto the mattress. She bounced, settled in atop the handmade quilt and then stared up at him through wide, whiskey-colored eyes.

He tore his clothes off, telling her, "I even stopped to bathe in the river so I wouldn't have to waste time with a damn shower once I got home."

She grinned and pushed herself up onto her elbows. "Must have been cold."

He shook his head. "Didn't feel a thing."

Then he was on the bed with her, pushing her nightgown up and over her head, baring her luscious breasts to his gaze, to his touch. He bent over her, took first one nipple then the other into his mouth, licking, nibbling, sucking, and felt her fingers thread through his hair, holding him in place.

His hands moved over her skin, fingers dipping below the elastic band of her panties, a tiny scrap of white lace. With one quick move, he snapped that band and tugged the lace free of her body. Then he touched her, covering her heat with the palm of his hand, feeling her body arch into him and listening to the soft sighs of expectation sliding from her lips.

"Jericho..."

"First time's going to be hot and hard, baby," he muttered against her breast. "I've been waiting for you too long."

"Yes," she said and met his gaze when he lifted his head. "Now, please. Fill me. I need you so much."

He didn't need to hear more. Jericho shifted position, knelt between her legs, then parted her thighs. He stroked her most sensitive skin with the tips of his fingers until she was writhing helplessly beneath him.

"Jericho, now..."

"Almost," he told her, watching her squirm, watching a passion-induced haze slide over her eyes.

Then, when he was satisfied that she was on the teetering brink of completion, he pushed his body into hers.

She gasped, lifting her hips to accommodate him, and he took advantage of her move, sliding ever deeper inside her. Her tight, hot body surrounded his and he groaned aloud at the sweeping satisfaction of finally being exactly where he'd dreamed of being.

This was all he had craved. This was what he needed above all else. Daisy. With her hot welcome, with her warm sighs and the soft ease of her lush body.

He levered himself over her, hands on either side of her head, and their eyes met and locked as he pumped himself into her. Plunging, claiming, again and again, his hips rocked against hers.

Her arms came around his neck, she locked her legs around his waist and pulled him deeper, tighter on every thrust. Breath mingled, mouths met and tongues twisted.

And when at last she tore her mouth from his and screamed his name, Jericho shouted in victory and allowed his body to explode into a pleasure so profound, it left him shattered.

Eight

They'd been at it for hours.

He was insatiable, Daisy thought with an inward smile. And very creative. Her body felt used and complete and was practically humming with stored energy. There was just something about incredible sex that made her feel strong enough to move mountains.

But even as that thought slid through her mind, she knew it was more. Knew that this long, incredible night had been about much more than simple sex. This wasn't just a case of needs being met, hungers assuaged. This was something else.

And that worried her.

She hadn't planned on loving Jericho.

But it seemed, she told herself, that it was too late to avoid it.

His body covering hers, she ran her hands up and down his spine, loving the hard, warm feel of his skin against hers. His breath puffed across her throat and their heartbeats thundered in time.

She'd gone to King Mountain because of his connection with her brother. Because she'd felt that Jericho and the military owed her one. They'd taken her brother—her only family—from her and she'd come to collect on that debt. But now, it was so much more complicated than that. She'd come to care for him and during the long, sex-fueled night, she'd taken that last trembling step into love.

Which left her exactly *where?*

"You're thinking," he murmured against her

skin. "I can practically hear the wheels in your head spinning."

She smiled and moved her hands up to thread through his hair. "Well, maybe you could think of something to do that would completely shut down my brain."

He lifted his head and grinned down at her. "Is that a challenge?"

"Do you need one?"

"Nope." He kissed her then slid his body down along hers, pausing along the way to taste her nipples, to run his tongue across her abdomen.

Daisy shivered as he moved over her, then she tipped her head back into the pillow as he knelt between her legs and lifted her hips from the bed. Her legs dangled and her hands fisted on the sheets as he lowered his mouth to her.

She watched him as he took her. As his mouth covered her and his tongue worked over that erotically charged bud of flesh. Again and again, he caressed that spot, sending tingles shooting through her system with complete abandon. His

breath was hot, his tongue was wicked and as
he took her, his hands kneaded her bottom until
she was besieged with too many sensations to
count.

Her heartbeat was frantic as she lay helplessly
in his strong grasp. She rocked her hips into his
mouth, claiming as much as she could of what
he was doing to her. His eyes burned into hers
and she couldn't look away. Couldn't tear her
gaze from his as the world around her splintered
and she called his name out one more time, her
throat sore, her voice raspy.

And before the last of the tremors had rocked
through her body, Jericho sat back on his heels,
grabbed her up and settled her over his throb-
bing erection. In one fluid move, she sheathed
him. Her arms went around him, her legs locked
about his waist and his big hands were at her
hips. He moved her on him, up and down, sliding into a hot friction that seemed to explode
into flames that enveloped them both.

He caught her mouth with his and this time,

when she called his name, he swallowed the sound and buried it under his own groan of completion.

Over the next few days, life on the mountain settled into a routine. A constantly changing routine in Jericho's opinion, but he seemed to be the only one bothered by it.

Daisy was imprinting herself not only on him, but also on his home. Clients arrived, were taken care of and left. Meals were not only healthier, but tastier, plus there was a variety that Kevin had never managed. She had become a part of the unit that lived and worked at the lodge. It was almost as if she'd always been there, and Jericho noticed that the guys spent a lot more time smiling than they used to.

Of course he noticed, because his frequent scowl was such a contrast.

Now, he walked into the great room and stopped on the threshold. Glancing around, he noted all the changes she'd made here, too.

Nothing was safe from the woman. Daisy had raided the attic, where generations of King clutter were stored and she'd found what she called "treasures." Handmade quilts done by Jericho's grandmother and decorative pillows that Daisy had strewn across the utilitarian furniture. The room had a softer feel now, with scattered rugs and splotches of color dotting the area.

"She's nesting," he muttered and waited for the zing of panic to shoot through him. But it didn't come.

Why?

Was he getting so used to having her around that he didn't mind the fact that she'd taken his well-ordered male world and turned it on its head? Was he so enthralled by the nights they spent together that he no longer worried about getting too attached? If that were the case, it was time to put the brakes on.

Because no matter how much he enjoyed her, being with her, the bottom line was she didn't belong. And she wouldn't last. One hard winter would be enough to send the city girl screaming back down the mountain in search of sidewalks and coffee shops.

He scowled at the thought and knew that when she was gone, it wouldn't be easy on him. He'd miss her, damn it, which was something he hadn't counted on. Best to start preparing himself for it now, he supposed.

"Hi," she said from right behind him. "You're back early. I thought you said you were going up the mountain today to check the fencing on the ridgeline."

"I did," he said and stepped aside so she could pass. But she didn't move away. Instead, she inched in closer to him. Close enough that he caught the ripe peach scent of the shampoo she preferred. Close enough that he felt waves of heat reaching out for him and his body responded in an instant.

He'd thought that getting Daisy into his bed would be the one sure way to get her *out* of his system. Hadn't worked out that way. Rather than chasing her out of his mind, sex with Daisy had burned her into his brain. One whiff of her scent, one touch of her hand could have him hard as iron and as eager as a teenager in the backseat of a car.

Focus, he told himself. Focus on anything but her. Not as easy as it sounded. "We've got three lawyers showing up tomorrow. Everything ready?"

She gave him a half smile, filled with confusion at his sudden brisk tone, but said, "Yes, their rooms are ready and I've got their dietary requirements. I had Tim drive down the mountain to get a few groceries today, but—"

He held up one hand to stop the flow of words and asked, "Tim? I told him to check the climbing wall today, make sure it was sound after the last rain."

"Sam did that," she said, moving past him to plump pillows and toss them onto the couch again. "He said he didn't mind and Tim was eager to make the trip. Something about stopping to say hello to his mom while he was in town..."

The reins of control were slipping out of his fingers and Jericho fought to get a firmer grip. "If I'd wanted Sam out slogging his way through the mud, I would have sent him."

Daisy turned around to face him. "What are you angry about?"

"Oh, I don't know," he said, tossing both hands high before letting them slap down against his thighs. "Maybe because I give orders that you change around to suit yourself?"

"Orders?"

Her voice sounded tight, but he was past caring. This was just a symptom, he told himself. Just one more sign that she was changing everything on him. She even had his men doing her bidding and forgetting all about whatever it was *he'd* told them to do. Well, it was time to remind her who was the boss around here.

"Yes, orders. You work for me, Daisy, not the other way around."

"I didn't say different, did I?"

"You didn't have to," he countered. "You do whatever the hell you want around here and expect the rest of us to just go along."

"I haven't heard any complaining," she snapped, folding her arms over her chest in a classic position of self-defense.

"You are now." He closed the distance between them with a few long strides. "Sam's too old to be pushing through mud. But you didn't think about that, did you?"

"He's hardly in his dotage, Jericho."

"And that's your decision to make, is it?"

"No," she argued, "it was Sam's decision and he made it. You're making a huge deal over nothing," she said and tipped her head to one side as she stared up at him. "So what's really bothering you? It's not Tim going to the store. Or Sam fighting with mud. What is it, Jericho? Just say it."

He scraped one hand across his face and blew out a frustrated breath. "I run this camp my way, understand? Stop countermanding my orders and everything will be fine." He glanced around the room, waved one hand at the feminine touches she'd added and grumbled, "And quit trying to girlie the place up while you're at it."

"Girlie?"

"Pillows, rugs, blankets…" He stopped and muttered, "Hell, it's getting to the point where I don't know what to expect every time I come into the room."

"Yes, well," Daisy said softly, "pillows and crochet work are dangerous entities…"

He snapped her an irritable look. "You know what I mean. Just do your job and nothing else."

"Uh-huh. Am I supposed to salute, too?"

"Wouldn't hurt!"

"You are the most impossible man," she said, shifting so that her hands were fisted on her hips. "Are you really that threatened by a few throw pillows and crocheted afghans? Do scented candles throw you into a tizzy?"

"This is still my house," he argued, even though he was beginning to feel like a damn fool.

"Nobody said it wasn't," she told him. "So why don't you tell me what's really bugging you, Jericho? You're not afraid of me, are you? Afraid I'm getting too close?"

The fact that that was *exactly* what was worrying him only irritated him further. His head snapped up and his gaze fired into hers. Gritting his teeth, he hissed in a breath and said, "Nobody gets any closer to me than I want them to be. So if you're looking at me and seeing rainbows and picket fences, then you need to get your eyes checked."

Rather than being put off by his gruff voice, barely restrained temper and crappy attitude, Daisy smiled at him. Her eyes lit up and she shook her head as she walked toward him. Then laying both palms flat on his chest, she went up on her toes and brushed her mouth across his.

"I see you clearly, Jericho. I always have."

Temper drained away from him as if someone had pulled a plug. Hard to maintain anger when you were straddling a razor blade of desire and want. "I'm not the kind of man you need."

"That's where you're wrong," she said softly with another sly smile. "You're exactly the man I need."

When she went into his arms, Jericho held her tightly to him, and he had to wonder if she'd be saying these things if she knew that he still blamed himself for her brother's death.

A couple of days later, it was a cloudy afternoon with a chilly bite to the air as Jericho packed up his truck for an annual fishing trip with his brothers Jesse and Justice. While he worked, Jericho actively wished both of his brothers to the other side of the planet. For the past two days, Jericho had been treating Daisy as if she were a land mine with a tricky trigger mechanism. He wasn't sure why. It wasn't as if the woman had a short fuse or anything. She was usually so damn happy it was hard to spot a frown on her face. But his tension had been bleeding into her and now she was wary, as if she was no longer sure just how to treat him.

Ever since that confrontation in the great room, neither one of them was entirely comfortable around the other.

You're exactly the man I need.

Her words repeated over and over again in his mind, making him short-tempered and more irritable than usual. What the hell had she meant? She needed him? For what?

Sex?

Or had she meant something more? Was she building castles in the air around him? Because if she was, they were going to collapse. He couldn't be the man for her. There were too many secrets between them. Too many things left unsaid, and once she knew the truth, he knew he'd never see that smile of hers again. Never feel her squirming beneath him in the middle of the night.

And that was a hell of a thing, wasn't it? He'd begun keeping his secret to protect her. Now, wasn't he just protecting himself? Wasn't he keeping the truth from her so that he wouldn't lose what he'd found with her?

This never should have begun, he thought. Going down this road was a mistake from the first and he'd known it. Hadn't he tried to get her to leave? Hadn't he tried to keep his distance? Hell, he'd realized right away that nothing good could come of this, but Daisy Saxon was a damn force of nature. She was unstoppable. Irresistible. He couldn't regret what he'd had with her the past few weeks, but he knew the memories of this time with her would haunt him for years after she was gone.

So what kind of bastard was he, to know all of this and still go to her bed every night?

"Idiot," he muttered darkly and tossed a folding

lawn chair into the bed of the truck. "Keep your distance, but don't stop sleeping with her."

But damned if he could stop himself. What was a man supposed to do? Turn his back on a warm, beautiful, *willing* woman who wanted him as much as he wanted her?

Guilt threatened to rear up inside him, but he pushed it away. Daisy was here because she wanted to be. The fact that she didn't know the whole truth of her brother's death meant nothing. There wasn't a thing he could do to change reality and didn't know if he would if given the chance. Of course, he would spare her pain, but would he take away her brother's bravery? Brant's decision to volunteer for dangerous duty, just to keep him safe? No. He couldn't do that and honor the kid. And that young Marine deserved the honor he'd found in death. Hell, they all did.

What was really bugging him was that he hadn't told Daisy the whole story. When she'd asked about her brother's death, he'd dodged her.

Told her only the bare minimum. Why? To save her grief? Or was it to save himself from having to see accusation shining in her whiskey eyes?

And did it matter? he demanded of himself silently. Was the reason important when the result was that he was hiding the truth? He, who put such store in honesty, was deliberately keeping something from the woman who was dominating his every thought. So he had to wonder what was driving that. Concern for someone else or self-service?

But as his mind went round and round that question for what had to be the hundredth time, Jericho told himself to suck it up. To keep his mouth shut and to wait Daisy out. One day soon, she'd realize that he wasn't the man for her, that nothing was going to come of whatever it was that was between them…and she'd give up and go away.

Daisy? His mind argued. Daisy, who didn't know the meaning of the word *quit?* Fat chance.

His brothers' voices rushed to him on a cold wind and he shook his head and grumbled under his breath. He was in no mood for dealing with Justice and Jesse, but he didn't have a choice in the matter. Every year, his brothers came up to King Mountain for a weekend fishing trip, guys only, just before the onslaught of winter. It was out of season, but on private property they could fish all they wanted to. They never actually caught much, but it was a good chance for them all to sit and talk and catch up on each other's lives.

Any other time, he would have been looking forward to it. He'd missed quite a few of these trips when he was still in the military. Now that he was home, he wanted to reconnect with his family. He had to admit that Daisy had had a part in that, too. She'd reminded him all too often about just how important family was. And when she'd discovered that Jesse and Justice were coming for a fishing trip, she'd been excited at the idea of meeting his brothers.

And excitement for Daisy translated into cooking and baking. The kitchen was stocked now with every kind of food and dessert imaginable. She had been determined that the King brothers would feel welcome. Now, she was practically pushing all three of them out the door to get them started on their overnight trip.

Jericho had noticed his brothers noticing Daisy and had even caught an inquisitive glance or two being exchanged. He knew what they were thinking. That the last King brother had finally taken the plunge. Well, once they were at the lake, he'd just set them both straight on that score.

"This is great," Justice said, as he approached, letting his gaze roam over the property. "I like the changes you made to the big house."

"Thanks." Jericho jerked his head toward the barn. "I've got a new horse you should see, too."

"Yeah?"

His eyes lit up and Jericho almost laughed

aloud. Justice was the patient one of the bunch of brothers. He was quiet, thoughtful, withdrawn. But you show him a horse and the rancher in the man stood up and roared.

Damn, it was good to see them, he thought, even though their timing sucked.

"We're not here to look at horses—we're here to fish and drink beer," Jesse told them both, tossing a tackle box into the back of Jericho's truck. "Bella and Maggie are having a girls' night in at the ranch—said they're planning a big family get-together, all of the cousins, God help us—for Christmas and Justice's house-keeper, Mrs. Carey, is in hog heaven with both of the kids to look after. Justice and I barely escaped with our lives."

Jericho just shook his head at his youngest brother. A former professional surfer, Jesse now owned and operated King Beach, a sportswear and sports equipment company. He was also crazy in love with his wife and Joshua, their son. "Sounds dangerous."

"That's no joke," Justice said. "Yeah, Jesse's a little dramatic as always, but I can tell you, Maggie and Bella together…" He shuddered. "No man can stand against 'em. By the time we got out of there, the two of them were buried in discussions over menus and decorations and there was talk of having *us* stick around so we could help 'em decide things like…redecorating." He shook his head again at their narrow escape. "For some damn reason, Maggie figures we need to repaint the whole inside of the ranch for this shindig they're planning and Bella's right there with her."

"Too true," Jesse said. "She was showing me paint samples on the ride to the ranch and couldn't understand why I didn't give a damn about pomegranate or hydrangea for the breakfast room."

"It's white now. What's wrong with white, I ask you?" Justice demanded of no one. "Those women are on a roll and nothing's going to stop 'em. We're just lucky that Maura and Jefferson are safely in Ireland."

"Can't believe my brothers are such wimps. Letting their wives run the show."

"So says the single man," Jesse pointed out and reached down for the cooler. "Wait until it's your turn and then we'll talk."

"It's never going to be *my* turn, Jesse," Jericho told him firmly. "Not a chance in hell I'll tangle myself up in marriage with anyone. Saw too much misery in the Corps. Even good marriages can end in pain, and I'm not interested in that, thanks."

"Just what I said," Jesse told him. "That changed when I met Bella."

"It was Maggie for me," Justice said, then added, "Your time will come, Jericho."

"Don't count on it," he answered. "I like my life just the way it is. I'm not looking for anything permanent and I'm not husband and father material."

"Didn't think I was either," Jesse said. "But

now I'm married, with a son who makes me happy and Bella's pregnant again."

"And you're just now telling us?" Justice accused. "Congratulations, man. That's great news."

"Yeah." Jesse shook his head and gave them a bemused smile. "Who would have guessed a few years ago that I'd be so damn happy changing diapers?"

Even Jericho had to admit silently that he never would have pegged his surfing brother as the family type. But clearly, he was.

"Know just what you mean," Justice said with a grin. "Now that Maggie's pregnant again, looks like the Kings are having another population explosion."

"All right!" Jesse slapped his brother on the shoulder. "Now all we need is for Maura and Jefferson to make another one and for Jericho to get with the program."

Jericho shook his head. "For me, not a chance. For Jefferson and Maura, you might want to cut them some slack. Hell, Jensen's not even a year old, is he?"

"Neither's Joshua," Jesse pointed out. Then he asked, "So, how about it, Jericho? You really want to be the only King not working on the next dynasty?"

"One of us has got to stay sane, don't you think?"

"You always were a tough son of a bitch," Jesse said with a wide grin. "Not to mention too stubborn to know what's good for you." He hefted the cooler. "Damn, this thing weighs a ton. What's in it?"

"The bare essentials," Daisy announced from the back door. "There's beer, beer and, oh, just in case you get thirsty, some beer."

"My kind of picnic," Jesse said on a laugh.

She grinned back at him and for a second, Jericho felt like an outsider. He envied his brothers' easy way with Daisy. There were no undercurrents between them. No lingering sexual tension that ratcheted up every conversation they had. His guts were twisting and his mouth was dry just watching her.

She wore a dark green sweater with the collar of a white shirt poking out at the neck. Her jeans were worn, but clung to her legs like a lover's hands and she was wearing those boots she'd tried to wear on their survival trip. She looked damn good and had Jericho's heartbeat pounding so loud it was a wonder no one else could hear it.

He wondered, too, if she'd been there in time to hear him say he'd never marry anyone. Had she listened in to his brothers' talk about family and babies, and had she heard Jericho's refusal to be drawn into it all? He hadn't heard her open the door, so it was possible.

And though a part of him hoped she'd missed it, another part acknowledged that it might be easier all the way around, for both of them if she knew exactly where he stood on this.

Nine

"The other cooler has sandwiches." Daisy was talking to all of them, but her gaze remained on Jericho as she added, "Along with potato salad, macaroni salad, fried chicken and chocolate-chip cookies."

"Ma'am," Justice said and swept his Stetson off as he bowed, "you are a gift from above and we thank you."

"No pasties?" Jericho asked, voice soft enough he half didn't expect her to hear him.

He should have known better. Her whiskey-colored gaze landed on him, but her smile was less than brilliant. Had she heard him talking to his brothers? Or was this simply a sign that she was going to miss him while he was gone?

"Pasties, too," she said, "since I know how much you like them."

There was one long, simmering second that flashed between them and it was as if his brothers weren't there. As if he and Daisy were alone on the mountain. And the depth of emotion rocking through him almost choked him. He hadn't counted on this, Jericho realized grimly. Hadn't counted on caring for her. The need for her had been so overpowering, he hadn't noticed when it became leavened with affection. With... Deliberately, he shut down that train of thought before it could leave the station.

He couldn't acknowledge, even to himself, that what he was feeling for her was anything more than a softening of a heart he hadn't realized was still there. What they shared wouldn't last. Couldn't.

Not only because, as he'd told his brothers, he wasn't looking for forever. But because there was still something she didn't know. He hadn't told her about Brant's last mission. Not yet. But, he told himself, that was exactly what he was going to have to do. As soon as he got back from this trip with his brothers, he'd be up-front with her. Tell her everything. Then she'd leave and things would get back to normal around here.

If he missed her the rest of his life, that was just something he'd have to deal with.

She laughed at something Jesse said and Jericho's gaze fixed on her. Everything inside him fisted up tight. The woman hit him on so many levels he couldn't even identify them all. He wanted her and at the same time wanted her gone. Needed her and resented that need. Cared for her, but fought against it at every breath.

How could one small, curvy woman instigate so many different emotions in a man? Especially one who'd made it his business to *never* feel deeply for anyone? Hell, until Daisy had stumbled into his life, the closest Jericho had come to commitment was the two weeks he'd spent at his cousin Rico King's hotel in Cancún, with a brunette he barely remembered.

For years, he'd carefully steered clear of entanglements, firmly believing that military life wasn't suited to hearth and home and family. He'd thought then and still did that a man served his country best when there were no other distractions in his life.

Jericho had seen too many families disintegrate under the strain of long deployments. Or worse yet, he'd seen the damage done to wives and kids when their Marine didn't make it home. His friends had insisted that he was looking at it all wrong, of course. They claimed the strength they got from their families more than made up for the worry of leaving them. And true enough, there were plenty of military personnel who made it work, balancing career and family so well they made it look easy.

But Jericho had drawn a firm line for himself.

He'd chosen to live a solitary life while in service.

What's your excuse now? a sly voice whispered in the back of his mind. He wasn't in the military anymore and still he kept people at a distance.

It was cleaner, he told himself. Less cluttered. Though those excuses sounded pitiful even to himself.

"So what's the big weekend plan?" Daisy was asking and Jericho came up out of his thoughts. Before he could speak though, Jesse was talking.

"To sit beside the lake and listen to my brothers' lies," he told her with a wink.

"The day you close your mouth long enough to listen to anybody will be the day they open an ice rink in hell," Justice told him, giving Jesse a friendly shove.

"Well now, you and Jericho are so damned close-mouthed, it only looks like I'm doing all the talking." He turned his smile on Daisy again. "You can testify to that, can't you, Daisy? Jericho's about as talkative as a rock, wouldn't you say?"

She turned her gaze on him and Jericho felt the solid punch of her stare. Humor shone in her eyes again as she said, "I don't know about that. He doesn't seem to have much trouble when he's telling me how he wants things run around here."

He scowled at her, but it was more for form's sake than anything else.

"Giving orders doesn't count," Jesse told her, leaning one hip against the back of the truck. "Because I'm the youngest, I can tell you I've been taking orders from my brothers since I first opened my eyes."

"Not that you ever follow them," Justice reminded him and lifted the heavy cooler filled with food so easily, it might have been empty. He set it in the back of the truck and glanced at Daisy. "His wife, Bella, came to my house just looking for a little peace and quiet."

"Ha!" Jesse laughed shortly, then got a be-mused look on his face. "My Bella? Peaceful? That'll be the day."

"Please," Justice said. "Your wife's a sweet-heart. You want to see a woman with a temper, you take my Maggie on in an argument. You'll be lucky to get out with your hide still attached."

"You're pitching Maggie's Irish temper against Bella's Mexican temperament?" Jesse laughed again. "No contest, big brother. Bella's small, but she's tough."

Both men continued to compare their wives, each of them sounding so damn proud of the women in their lives that Jericho felt a moment's envy. Which was new for him. He was even tempted to jump in and tell them both that Daisy was more woman than either of their wives.

That thought startled him down to the bone. Usually, all he experienced when his brothers started talking was a pang of sympathy for the women who'd chosen to love his hardheaded brothers. Now though, since Daisy, Jericho could understand just what his brothers felt for their wives. Didn't make him feel any better to realize it though. Instead, it seemed to solidify for him the fact that he'd let Daisy get too close.

He'd allowed her to *matter*.

Jericho stood to one side, his gaze still locked with Daisy's as his brothers ragged on each other. The banter was familiar and comfortable. The only difference this time was that Daisy was here, so Jericho's mind wasn't really on keeping up with his brothers. Instead, all he could think was that he wished the weekend was over so that he could drag her upstairs, lock the two of them up in his room and forget about everything but her for the next twenty-four hours or so.

Yes, he'd decided to tell her everything, his mind argued, but that wasn't saying he couldn't have one more night with her first. If that made him a selfish bastard, then he could live with that.

"Yo, Jericho!" Jesse punched his arm. "You alive?"

"Yeah, I am, little brother," he said, tearing his gaze from Daisy long enough to give Jesse a hard stare that had once been known to freeze Marine recruits in their tracks. Naturally enough, Jesse didn't even flinch. Disgusted, Jericho told him, "Load up the rest of the gear so we can get moving."

"See?" Jesse pointed out to no one, "Still giving orders."

"You guys have fun," Daisy said with a laugh as she headed down the back porch steps and turned for the corner of the house. "Come on, Nikki," she called to the little dog clearly torn between walking with her or staying to stare longingly at Jericho. "I've got some chrysanthemums to stake. Guess I'll see you all tomorrow night?"

"We'll be back by supper time," Justice assured her.

She lifted one hand and kept walking, disappearing around the edge of the log house, with the dog pausing for one backward look before joining her.

"Staking flowers?" Jesse muttered with a shake of his head as he looked after her. "Why?"

"Do I look like a gardener to you?" Jericho asked with irritation. "How the hell would I know?" He scrubbed one hand across his chin. "I didn't even know we had chrysanthemums."

Jesse turned to the task at hand, tossing in sleeping bags and a camp stove, then he carefully set their fishing poles into the back of the truck, too. While he worked, Jericho simply stared off into space, watching the spot where Daisy had vanished.

"Something you want to tell me?" Justice asked quietly as he stepped up alongside him.

"Huh?" Jericho started and looked at him as though he were crazy. But it wouldn't fool Justice. He'd always been the one of them to see things no one wanted him to see. Well, except when it came to his own life. Their oldest brother Jefferson had explained to Jericho just how badly Justice had screwed up his marriage to Maggie. And how close the couple had come to losing everything that was between them.

"I'm not blind, you know," Justice told him. "I can see how she looks at you—and just how you're looking back."

"You don't know what you're talking about." Damn it. He should have expected this, he told himself. Of course Justice would pick up on the tensions between him and Daisy. Of course he'd notice things Jericho would rather keep under the radar.

"Yeah? Then why is it you look like a man on the ragged edge?" Justice asked. "Hell, Jericho. You finally fall for a woman and you're not going to do anything about it?"

"Nobody fell for anybody," he argued, distinctly uncomfortable with the conversation.

"What's this?" Jesse sidled up alongside Justice and stuck his two cents in. "The Almighty Jericho King falling in love?" He laughed and reached out to shove Jericho's shoulder. "This is big news, man!"

"Will you shut the hell up?" Jericho snapped, shooting a glance at the spot where Daisy had last been seen just to make sure she wasn't in earshot. Now that Jesse had caught wind of this, there would be no keeping him quiet. "Nobody said anything about love."

"Didn't have to. Hell," Justice mused, "you practically set her on fire just looking at her."

"Lust isn't love, in case you didn't know that already," he told his brothers, sparing first one, then the other of them a hard glare meant to end the conversation once and for all. Of course, it didn't.

"It's a good start though," Jesse told him, his unabashed grin nearly splitting his features in two. "First time I saw Bella…" He paused for a heavily dramatic sigh, then said, "Well, not the first time. The first time, it was dark and I could hardly see her at all. The second time, she was wearing this ugly-ass tent dress, but the *third* time," he mused with a grin, "that's the one that got me."

"You're an idiot," Jericho told him. "And my sympathies to your wife."

Jesse's eyebrows lifted as he laughed, clearly unoffended. "She loves me."

"No accounting for taste," Justice put in.

"Hey," Jesse shot back, "we were ragging on Jericho, remember?"

"And now you're done. You talk too much," Jericho told him. "Always did. A bad habit you ought to try to break."

"Too late now," Jesse said with a negligent shrug. He walked back to the truck and took a seat on the tailgate. "Besides, it's part of my charm."

"Is that what that is?" Jericho lifted his gaze to the sky. They had a good four hours before sunset. Time enough to drive to the lake and set up camp. If he could get his brothers to back off and get moving. "So are we ready to go or what?"

"Changing the subject doesn't make anything go away, you know."

"I'm not changing the subject," he said tightly, with a glare for each of his brothers. "There is no subject because I'm not talking about it at all. Not with you two. Not with anyone. Because there's nothing to talk about."

"Are you crazy or just stupid?" Jesse asked from his perch on the tailgate. "A woman who not only looks like that and can cook *and* can stand being around your crab-ass attitude for longer than five minutes and you're not falling on your knees in front of her?"

Jericho sneered at him.

"He's over the top again," Justice said, with a little more heat in his voice than usual, "but Jesse's got a point. For God's sake, Jericho, you really want to spend the rest of your life a hermit on this mountain?"

"How am I a hermit? I've got people coming and going all the damn time."

"Key word there in that sentence," Jesse tossed in, *"going."*

Jericho snapped at him. "Who asked you to talk?"

Jesse pushed off the tailgate, stood up straight to face his older brother and said, "You ever notice that your attitude gets even crappier when you're wrong?"

"Just shut up, will you?" Jericho shook his head, looked at his more rational brother and asked, "Justice can I toss him in the lake?"

"You could try," Jesse goaded.

"Nah," Justice said, "Bella'd have a fit. And trust me when I say you don't want to see that woman angry."

"Amen," Jesse muttered.

"Fine. No tossing in lakes, but no more 'advice' from you either," Jericho said and slammed the gate of the truck shut with enough force to rattle metal.

"Fine," Jesse agreed. "No more advice, even though you really need it."

"Get in the truck," Justice told him, then when Jesse was gone, he said, "He's right, you know. About Daisy. And you. You might want to think about this before you screw something good up. I know. I damn near did the same thing myself."

Jericho sighed, shoved one hand through his hair and said, "I'm glad you and Maggie made it work. Really. But this thing with Daisy, it's different."

"How?"

"There are things she doesn't know," Jericho said. "Things we haven't talked about. But even discounting that...bottom line?" Jericho said with a slow shake of his head. "We're way too different. I'm scotch, she's wine. I'm outdoors, she's in. Just wouldn't work because, like it or not, she doesn't belong here."

Daisy bit down on her bottom lip to keep from speaking up and giving away her position. She should have known better than to stand there and listen in on Jericho and his brothers. And she really hadn't meant to at first. But when she'd headed back for the house to get a pair of scissors to use to deadhead the flowers, she'd gotten caught back up in their conversation.

It had been fun listening to the three brothers go back and forth, making fun, teasing each other. She'd been reminded of how she and Brant had talked and laughed together, so she'd stayed hidden, enjoying the easy banter between them.

Then, when the conversation had shifted to her, she'd been too intrigued to leave.

Now, anxiety wrapped itself around her and she felt cold to the bone. She leaned back against the side of the house and curled her hands into fists at her sides. It took everything she had to stand her ground and not go rushing out into the yard, demanding that Jericho tell her what he'd been keeping from her.

What was it she didn't know?

What was he hiding?

"And why?" she whispered, glancing briefly down at Nikki who sat, head cocked, ears lifted as if considering Daisy's question.

But when no answers came, Daisy shifted her gaze to stare up at the sky. She didn't see the clouds sweeping across that wide expanse. Instead, she saw Jericho's ice-blue eyes looking down at her. In her mind's eyes, she saw his face, emotion charging his features as he covered her body with his. As they lay together in the shadows, talking and laughing after the loving.

And she saw him now, as he'd faced Justice and said, *She doesn't belong here.*

How could he still believe that? Hadn't she made a place for herself here? Hadn't she helped him with his clients, turned his stark, barren house into a comfortable home? Hadn't she spent every night in his arms?

Irritation spiked inside her, warring instantly with the regret and sorrow that had her system strangling. He thought *she* was stubborn? They'd

spent every day of the past few weeks together.
Worked together. She'd gone on one survival
trip with him and his clients and not only had
she kept up, but she'd also handled the cooking
and made the camp's clients more comfortable.
She'd proved herself, she knew she had.

Yet, he still held back.

Still stood to one side and pronounced that she
didn't fit. Didn't belong. What would it take for
him to admit that she *did?* Or would he, ever?
If he was so determined to keep her out, would
that ever change? Wasn't she just setting herself
up for disappointment and pain if she remained,
waiting, hoping he'd see the light?

"This is your own fault," she muttered as she
listened to the rumble of the men's laughter. "If
you hadn't fallen for him, then this wouldn't
matter at all. You'd simply leave as you'd planned
to do in the first place and you wouldn't have
looked back."

But that was the trouble, she told herself. She
would be looking back. Always.

Jericho laughed aloud at something one of his brothers said and the rich, deep sound of it sliced into her.

Nikki whined and Daisy bent to scoop up the little dog and cuddle her close to comfort both of them. At the moment, she wanted nothing more than to walk right out there and confront Jericho. She wanted answers. She wanted him to look her in the eye and try to say she didn't belong. That there was nothing between them.

"This shouldn't have happened," she told herself quietly, her voice lost in the sigh of the wind. "Daisy," she murmured, burying her face in Nikki's soft fur, "why did you have to fall in love with him? Why couldn't you have just slept with him and kept your heart out of the mix?"

Too late to regret that now, she thought, as pain whipped through her. She wished she could see Jericho's face. Would she see the lie in his eyes? Or would she see an indisputable truth written there?

But she stood her ground, because as long as

he was with his brothers, it wasn't the time to confront him. She'd only look like the fool she felt for having been caught eavesdropping on them all.

She stayed put and waited until the truck engine fired up and the three men rode off down the long drive. Only then did she come around the edge of the house to look at the fantail of dust rising up in the wake of the truck.

Her heart ached as Jericho's words played over and over in her head. He was determined to feel nothing for her, she realized. It didn't matter that her own feelings had grown and changed since she'd first come to King Mountain. Didn't matter that she loved him—he wouldn't be interested.

She wrapped her arms around herself and held on, scraping her hands up and down her upper arms in a futile attempt to beat back the rising chill inside her. Until just a few minutes ago, she hadn't even been aware that she'd begun nursing dreams centered around Jericho. Dreams that had the two of them happily living together here on the mountain. Building a family. Raising their children and loving each other every night.

How hard it was to feel those nebulous dreams shatter and dissolve as if they'd never been. But through that pain, she managed to console herself with the fact that she'd done what she'd originally come here to do. She'd made love with Jericho King and if the gods were kind, she was already pregnant. She'd find out soon and then, while she still was able, she'd leave him here on his precious mountain and find another place to belong.

But not, she told herself, before she found out exactly what he was hiding from her.

Ten

By the end of the following week, Daisy felt as if her nerves were strung as tight as a newly tuned piano's strings. After his brothers left for home, Jericho had retreated into himself. He hadn't touched her, kissed her—had hardly *looked* at her in days. And the strain of that was beginning to take its toll. While she stood at her bedroom window looking out at the night, her mind raced even as she stood as if frozen in place.

Sensing a coming confrontation between her

and Jericho, Daisy had made a trip into the local town and found the pregnancy test she'd been looking for. But buying it didn't mean using it. The tidy blue box was still sitting in the cupboard beneath her bathroom sink, unopened.

She knew why she was hesitating to use it, of course. If she wasn't pregnant, then she'd be staying on, whether Jericho approved or not—she'd find a way to stay close. To fight his instincts to chase her off. If she was pregnant, then she could leave—just as he wanted her to. As she'd planned.

Which, she told herself sadly, was exactly why she hadn't used the test kit yet. She didn't want to go. Didn't want to leave Jericho, this place and the handful of employees that had given her such a feeling of family. She was a part of the life here now. She'd become one of them. She'd found her place in the world, found the one man she wanted above all others and she didn't want to lose any of it.

Giving up went against her very nature, she

thought. But was it giving up to leave when that had been the original plan? And was it worth it to stay if Jericho never allowed himself to care for her? God, her head hurt.

"What're you doing?"

Nikki yipped in excitement from her perch on the bed and Daisy spun around to face Jericho when he spoke up from the doorway to her bedroom.

"Nothing," she blurted because he'd caught her off guard and at a vulnerable moment. She forced a smile that felt brittle and false. "Just thinking."

He walked into the room and didn't stop until he was no more than an arm's reach away. He ignored Nikki, who pranced to the edge of the bed, hoping for a scratch and head rub.

"I've been doing some thinking, too," he said and he didn't look any happier with his thoughts than she was with hers.

The time had come. Everything inside Daisy braced for whatever was next.

When silence spun out between them, Daisy took it for as long as she could and then felt what little patience she had left splinter and blurted, "For heaven's sake, Jericho, just say it."

His dark brows drew together and his mouth flattened into a grim line. "Say what?"

"What you came here to say," she challenged. "What you've been dying to say since the day I arrived. You want me to leave the mountain."

"You're wrong," he ground out. Shoving one hand through his hair, he stalked past her, looked out the window and, after a long minute, swiveled his head to lock his gaze with hers. "I don't want you to go..."

Her heart swelled and an instant later deflated as if someone had popped it with a needle.

"...which is why you have to."

She blinked at him, shook her head and finally managed to say, "That makes absolutely no sense."

"Doesn't have to," he told her flatly. "Like I said before, my mountain, my rules."

So cold. So hard. So distant. Not the man she'd come to know at all. He was already pulling away so fast she could hardly reach him. And that tore at her.

"So I'm supposed to just leave. Without an explanation. Without— Why, Jericho? Do I worry you that much?"

He laughed shortly, but there was no humor in the sound. "You don't worry me, Daisy. You just have to go."

"Why?"

"Don't make this harder than it has to be," he told her.

"Oh, I think I will." As she said it, as her spine stiffened and her shoulders squared, she realized that she was going to fight to stay, not even knowing if she was pregnant or not, she was going to take a stand. Because looking up into his ice-blue eyes, Daisy knew he was something worth fighting for. What they had together was too important to let die without a battle.

He looked like the cold-eyed warrior he was,

she thought. But her brother had been a Marine, too. Now, Jericho was about to realize that this Saxon could be just as tough as any combat-hardened Marine.

And she fired her biggest gun with her first salvo.

"I love you."

His features went blank and, if possible, his eyes became even icier, more remote. "No, you don't."

Anger, hot and alive, pumped through her and she stepped right up to him. Tipping her head back so she could give him a full power glare, she said, "You might think you know everything, Jericho King, but you do not get to tell me what I do and don't feel. I said I love you. And I meant it. Now you have to deal with it."

She didn't have to wait long for his response and, frankly, it was pretty much just what she had expected.

"You think I'm blind, Daisy?" He countered, looming over her. His voice was low, rough and sounded as if the words were being ripped from his soul. "You think I don't see what's really going on? It's not me you love. It's being here, with me, with Sam and the others. You've been lonely since your brother died and now you've made us the family you want back so badly."

She felt as if he'd slapped her. Perhaps there was some truth in his words, but it wasn't the whole picture, not by a long shot. Yes, she'd come here looking to find a family again. She hadn't expected to find love, but she had. And she wouldn't let him make that less than it was.

Honestly. She told him she loved him and he threw her feelings back in her face? What kind of man did something that stupid?

"You idiot. Do you really believe I'm that big a simpleton? Do you think I don't know the difference between love and longing?" She fisted her hands at her hips and leaned in, narrowing her gaze on him until her eyes were mere slits of fury. "Of course I was lonely. But I didn't just pick the first man I ran into to become the family I miss so much. I came here because you knew my brother. I didn't come looking for a husband or someone to cling to. I don't cling. I didn't mean to fall for you. It just... happened."

He frowned, but she wasn't finished.

"Of all the arrogant, foolish, stubborn men in the world, why is it you I had to fall in love with?" Shaking her head, she reached up and yanked at her own hair in frustration. "You're so determined to lock yourself away up on this mountain, shut away from anything or anyone who might matter to you that you absolutely refuse to see that not only do I love you, but you love me back!"

He took a step away, ground his teeth together so hard she could see a muscle in his jaw twitch. She watched as he fought for control and finally managed it. Only then did he speak.

"You know, I didn't ask for this. Didn't want it." He blew out a breath. "You're the one who showed up and wouldn't go away. You're the one who kept pushing and prodding me until I was in a corner."

"Poor you," she said with a slow shake of her head.

A smirk curved his mouth briefly. "Justice and Jesse don't know squat about tough women," he said. "You could give their wives lessons."

"Thank you."

"Not sure it was a compliment."

"I am. I'm not afraid to say what I want. To fight for what I want. Are you?"

He inhaled sharply, deeply. "If a man said that to me, I'd punch him," he admitted.

"Really?"

He didn't respond to that. "I made up my mind before I left with my brothers that when I came back, I was going to take you to bed and keep you there for twenty-four straight hours and then I was going to send you away. For your own good."

She rocked in place, shaken by his words. "But you haven't so much as touched me in days."

"Because when I got back and saw you again… I knew that if I touched you I'd never let you go. And I have to let you go."

Something small and sharp seemed to tear at her heart. "Why?"

He shook his head.

"There are things you don't know…"

"So tell me," she countered.

He scrubbed one hand across his face.

"Honestly, Jericho, does the thought of being loved really engender so much panic?"

"Not panic, no," he told her honestly, the shutters in his eyes lifting slightly, the ice there melting just enough for her to see a glimmer of warmth shining out at her. "But second thoughts, even third…yes. You don't know what you're doing."

"You're wrong." She walked toward him, one deliberate step after another.

He stood his ground. Not backing away. Not

turning from her. Just watching her with a fire in his eyes that melted the last of her anger and fueled another emotion entirely.

"No, I'm not," he said softly, gaze locked with hers as she approached. "If you knew what was good for you, you'd pack up your stuff and be off the mountain inside an hour."

"I'm not going anywhere."

"To tell the truth, never thought you would," he admitted and swallowed hard as he reached for her. "I may be damned for this one day, but God help me, I can't let you go. Won't let you go."

"What're you saying?" she whispered.

"I'm saying that right here, right now, I need you." He took a breath. "Not talking about a future or happily ever after. Don't ever count on a future. Right now is all I can offer."

"Then for now," she said, "that's all I'll ask for."

Jericho's arms came around her like a vise, holding her to him, pressing her body's length along his. She buried her face in the curve of his neck as he clung to her and he felt her warmth slide into him, filling all the cold, empty places he'd been living with for days.

She loved him and he was going to let her. For however long it lasted, he would take what she so wanted to give and give her what he could in return. He'd never thought of himself as the "forever" kind of man, but he knew that for right now, he was where he belonged. With the woman he wanted above all else.

When he cupped her face with his palm and turned her mouth up to his, he kissed her with a depth that left him hungry for what he found only with her. But an instant later, that moment was shattered by a single shout from outside.

"Fire!"

The barn was burning and the next few hours passed in a blur.

Heat, shifting light thrown by wind fed writhing flames, the shouts of men and the screams of terrified horses filled the night air. Jericho directed his men, shouting orders over the noise. The volunteer fire department had been called out, but no one was standing around waiting. Hoses were dragged from every area of the yard, and water was aimed at the flames licking along the sides and climbing toward the roofline of the barn.

They fought to get the fire under control to prevent it from spreading not only to the other buildings but to the forest itself. It had been a long dry summer and the only thing they had going for them was the fact that it had recently rained.

The crackle and hiss of the fire sounded like demons chattering in the shadows. And that was what it felt like as well—as if hell had come to the mountain. The heat was amazing and Jericho felt sweat pouring down his back as he made run after run into the barn, leading the horses out. The terrified animals refused to cooperate, so the process took far longer than it should have.

But he was intent on getting every animal out of the barn alive.

Just as he'd been intent on keeping Daisy safe.

"Stay in the house!" he'd shouted at her when the first call for help had sounded out. Immediately, he'd raced away from her, fully expecting her to hear and *obey* him, for God's sake.

Naturally, she didn't.

She paused only long enough to close the bedroom door, making sure Nikki couldn't get out and be injured, then she was on his heels as he ran downstairs for the front door. Before he could shout at her again, she'd yelled, "Don't waste your breath, Jericho. This is my home, too, and I'll help save it."

Then she had bolted out of the house and he'd had no choice but to follow after her. Still he'd kept as close an eye on her as possible throughout the battle with the fire.

She was tireless, he thought as the mountain

fire department roared up the drive and more men joined the struggle. Daisy handled one of the ranch garden hoses, shooting streams of water on the flames as the men beat at the fire with wet blankets. She never quit. Never flagged. She stood her ground alongside the others and faced whatever fears were choking her without once turning from them.

And as the night wore on and sparks flew into the night, winking from brilliance to darkness, Jericho at last realized the truth.

He loved her.

Loved her with everything he was.

It wasn't about lust. Wasn't about not wanting her to go. It was so much more. He'd tried to tell himself she was just a clumsy, pretty city girl. But there was grit and strength and purpose in her. She was the woman for him.

The only woman.

By the time the fire was contained, Daisy was in the kitchen making boatloads of coffee for the men. Jericho found her there, face sooty, clothes grimy, her hair tangled—and he thought she'd never looked lovelier to him.

"More coffee's on the way," she said, with a quick glance at him.

"That's good. The men are sucking it down as fast as you take it out there."

"Fire's really out?"

"Completely," he said, walking to her, laying his hands on her shoulders and turning her around to face him. "Fire chief thinks it was an electrical thing. Started in one of the wall panels. But we got lucky." He pulled her in close, wrapped his arms around her and felt himself settle for the first time in what felt like forever. "No one was hurt. The animals are safe and we'll rebuild the barn. Structure's still sound. Just going to take—"

"A coat of paint?" she murmured wryly.

He chuckled, kissed the top of her head and said, "A little more than that, but it'll be good."

"And I'll be here to see it?" She tipped her

head back and looked up at him. "No more talking about me leaving?"

"No," he told her, wiping away some of the grime from her cheek with the pad of his thumb. "I don't want you to go. Ever."

She smiled at him. "That's the nicest thing you've ever said to me, Jericho King. But you already said it before."

"This is...different. I've got plenty more to say, Daisy Saxon," he admitted. "Starting with—"

"Don't."

The proposal that had leaped to the tip of his tongue stayed locked inside when she shushed him by laying her fingertips against his mouth. Confusion rushed through him. Hell, he knew she'd guessed what he was about to say—so why did she stop him? "Daisy..."

"Before you say anything else, there's something I have to tell you," she whispered.

From outside came the clatter and noise of the men working to put away the firefighting equipment and getting the animals settled down again. They'd have to put the horses up in one of the outbuildings for the night. It wouldn't be a long-term solution but for right now… Jericho dragged his mind back from the logistical problems facing him and instead focused on the woman watching him with a wary regret in her eyes.

"What is it?" His voice was low, his chest tight with the pressure of his breath backing up in his lungs. "What's wrong?"

"Nothing's wrong," she assured him and took a deep breath herself, as if trying to find her own balance before continuing the conversation. "But I have a feeling you were about to ask me to marry you…"

"And you don't want to marry me?" Shock pumped through him. Daisy, the woman to whom commitment was essential? The woman who longed for family was now going to turn down a proposal from the man she claimed to love? This had to be the weirdest situation he'd ever found himself in.

Jericho had never considered proposing to anyone before. Now that he was ready, the woman he loved was heading him off before he could say the words? What the hell was going on? "You said you love me."

"I do," she said quickly. Reaching up, she cupped his face in her hands and speared her gaze into his. "Oh, Jericho, I do love you. Completely. But I can't marry you until I'm completely honest with you. I think we both need to be truthful with each other. So I'll go first. I can't let you ask me the question until you know the real reason I came here."

"What?" The tension in the kitchen was alive and pulsing around them. So Jericho did what he always had when faced with a problem. He charged right at it. "What do you mean, the real reason?"

She blew out a breath, squared her shoulders and said, "I came here planning to seduce you, Jericho. I wanted a baby and I wanted *you* to be the father."

Eleven

Everything in him went cold and still.

It was as if he were standing outside himself, a silent observer to a scene that had him both furious and baffled.

"You what?"

When she pulled back from him, he let her go. It was better to keep a distance right now. He didn't know what he was feeling and his brain was racing from one thought to another.

"I wanted a family, Jericho," she said, filling a thermos with the freshly brewed coffee. Her hands weren't entirely steady though, and some of the hot, dark liquid spilled onto the countertop. "Brant was all I had. When I lost him…" She stopped, capped the thermos and turned to him. "I was crazy with grief for so long. Weeks, months, all I could do was mourn him. Mourn the loss of my family. When I finally came up for air and realized that I needed to keep living, I knew I didn't want to live alone."

He didn't know what to say to that so he held his silence and waited. It didn't take her long to continue.

"You called me, remember?"

He nodded.

"You offered to help me for the sake of Brant. Because of the connection you two had had."

"Yeah, but I don't remember offering you a child."

She flushed and even through the grime and soot on her face, Jericho could see the pink stain color her skin. "No, you didn't. That was my idea. Don't you see? The Marine Corps stole my family. Brant died for his country, but with him gone, I was so alone. I hated it. It tore at my heart until I thought I would die from the pain."

Something inside him softened toward her. He knew what it was to experience loss. Hell, he'd seen grief destroy people. The fact that Daisy had not only risen above it but found the strength to go on was admirable. But that didn't explain the rest of it. Then she was talking again and Jericho told himself to listen.

"When I decided to have a child, I knew I wanted you to be the father," she admitted. "You and Brant were friends. He admired you so much. And frankly, I thought, Jericho King is part of what took Brant from me—so what could be better than having you be the father of my new family?"

"I don't believe this," he muttered, rubbing the back of his neck hard enough to tear off a layer of skin. When his gaze snapped to hers it was hard and brutal. "So all of this was a scheme? You've been playing me from the start?"

Before she could say anything, he answered his own question on a short laugh. "Of course you have. Damn me, I was sucked in, too. I actually believed you were exactly who you said you were. Hell," he added, throwing his hands high and wide, "I even felt bad for 'taking advantage of you.' There's a joke."

"Jericho, let me explain—"

"No," he said sharply. "Answer one question. Did your plan work? Are you pregnant?"

She took a deep breath and folded her hands across her middle as if already protecting something precious. "Yes. I took the test when I came in to make the first batch of coffee."

"Bullshit," he said. "We used protection."

"Not the first night."

Jericho's world rocked precariously around him. His mind raced back to that first night when he'd come home to her and had been blinded by everything but the staggering hunger rampaging through him. No, he hadn't used a condom. Hell, he'd been doing good to find the damn bed. He'd been blind for her. Conscious only of the need pounding in his veins.

So he couldn't blame her entirely. He wanted to, God knew, because she'd tricked him. She'd made him believe. Made him trust and now she had shown herself as a liar.

"That's perfect," he muttered, turning from her to stare out the window at the men still working in the compound. From upstairs came Nikki's frantic barks and yips as she demanded to be freed from captivity. And behind him stood a woman who was carrying his child.

"Jericho—"

"What the hell am I supposed to do with this?" he asked and didn't really expect an answer.

"I'm sorry I lied to you," she said softly, "but I'm not sorry I came here. I was looking to find a family and instead I found *love*." She took another breath and added, "Jericho, everything changed for me after I'd been here just a few days. I knew then that it wasn't just a child I wanted. I wanted *you*. I love you."

He snorted. "Handy. How you confess your love for me right after you find out you're pregnant."

"I told you before I knew."

He laughed again. "And of course I believe you."

"Why are you so angry?" she asked, taking a step toward him. "Because I lied to you or because I'm pregnant?"

Jericho didn't have the answer to that. He could hardly believe that he was going to be a father, for God's sake. That was a hard piece of truth to hand a man. Wasn't he allowed a few minutes to take it in? To try to decide what he was feeling?

"I'm not talking about this now," he muttered and snatched up the thermos she'd prepared. He turned and headed for the back door, but her voice stopped him before he could leave.

"Jericho, I'm not the only one with secrets.

And nothing's changed. I still love you. And you love me."

He looked into her eyes and saw worry glittering in those whiskey-colored depths. But he couldn't assuage it. Couldn't give her what she needed. Not right now. "I don't even know you," he said and walked out to rejoin the men.

The next morning, he was gone.

She'd spent the night alone in her room, with only Nikki for company. She felt cold and lost and when she caught herself blindly reaching for him across an empty bed, the tears came.

How had this all become so confused? So twisted inside and out? In the long, sleepless hours of the night, Daisy had had time to think. To realize that she'd never really considered how her plan would affect Jericho.

Stupid, she knew, but in her quest to have a family, to become pregnant, she'd never stopped to think how her decision would affect him.

Three days later, Jericho was still gone and

Daisy was no closer to figuring out exactly what it was she should do next. Walking into the kitchen, Nikki right alongside her, she put one hand to her abdomen and thought about the child already growing inside her.

Soon, she would have a baby. A family. But would that family ever be complete without her child's father?

Nikki walked to the door, sat down and stared at it. Just as she had since Jericho left, as if she could make him appear with the power of her mind. Funny, Daisy thought, she and her dog were in the same boat. Both of them missing the only man either of them wanted.

The back door opened suddenly and she started, gaze shifting quickly, heartbeat accelerating, stomach pitching with an infusion of hope. Nikki yipped in excitement, then drooped to the floor. Daisy knew just how she felt. The expectation she'd felt so briefly drained away as Sam stepped into the room. He must have seen the disappointment she felt written on her face because he gave her a wry smile.

"Sorry," he said as he closed the door behind him. His eyes were kind and an understanding smile curved his mouth. "You don't have to worry about him, you know. He does this occasionally."

"Does what?" she asked. "Disappear?"

He shrugged and answered, "Yeah. You know that. He'll go up into the high country whenever he feels things closing in on him. Sometimes he's gone for days, sometimes longer."

"Longer." Fabulous. How would she ever last without seeing him? Talking to him? Making him listen to her? Jericho was a former Marine. He knew all about survival and getting by in the woods with no more than a piece of string and a knife. He could stay gone for weeks.

"It's none of my business what's going on between the two of you," Sam said softly, "but whatever it is, you'll work it out."

"Not if he doesn't come back."

"He'll be back."

"I wish I was so sure," she told him, moving across the room toward the refrigerator. She opened it, pulled out a bottle of water and opened it. After a long drink, she admitted, "He's furious, Sam. What if he doesn't come back?"

The older man gave her a smile. "He will. This is home. He's never been able to stay away too long. Besides, he loves you."

"I don't know about that."

"Well, I do," Sam said and walked to the coffeepot. Getting down a heavy mug, he poured himself a cup, took a sip and sighed. Then he continued, "I've known Jericho for years and I've never seen him the way he is with you."

That was something, Daisy thought, hope beginning to rise inside her again. If Sam had seen something in Jericho change and grow, then maybe what they'd found together would be strong enough to get past what she was sure Jericho saw as a betrayal.

Oh, God, she had betrayed him. Hadn't meant

to, but she could see now how it would feel to Jericho. How he might not be able to trust her. How he might think she was using him. And how could she change his mind if he didn't come back?

"Thank you," she said, taking a seat at the high breakfast bar. Late morning light spilled through the windows, dazzling against the appliances. Outside, the sounds of construction rang out. Hammers, saws and the shouts of men as they worked together rebuilding the damaged section of the barn.

"That means a lot to me, Sam. But the truth is, I really hurt him. I didn't mean to, but I did just the same."

"He's a big boy with thick skin. He'll get over it."

"I hope you're right."

"Usually am," he said with a quick grin. Then his features sobered and he stared down into his coffee for a long moment before he looked at her again. "I haven't said this to you before, but you coming here was a good thing, Daisy."

"I'd like to think so," she admitted. It would make her own sense of guilt much easier to bear. God, she kept seeing the flash of emotion in Jericho's eyes and it all but choked her. She'd been so happy when she saw the positive pregnancy test. So pleased that she'd gotten her wish. That she was carrying Jericho's baby.

Then, when she was sure he was going to propose, she hadn't been able to let him go through with it. Not without telling him the truth. Now she didn't know what to do. What to feel. She had her baby, but had she lost Jericho forever?

"How can it be a good thing," she said quietly, "if my coming here has made him so miserable?"

"Everybody gets mad, honey. Can't go through life without wanting to kick the furniture once in a while. But I've noticed that the only people who can really set us off are the ones who matter."

"You think?"

"I'm not the only one who's noticed the change in Jericho, you know." He locked his eyes with hers as if trying to impress upon her just how important what he was about to say was to him. "He's easier with everyone. Like a heavy weight's been lifted off his shoulders. When your brother died, it tore him up some."

Tears welled in her eyes at the mention of Brant and the reminder that her brother and the man she loved had once been close. "I know they were friends."

"They were," Sam agreed. "But it was more than that. As often happens to those who serve together, Jericho and Brant became more brothers than friends. Suppose he already told you how hard it hit him when that kid died. Guess you know how Jericho struggled for a long time with wondering whether he might have prevented Brant's death."

A ball of ice dropped into the pit of her stomach. "Prevented it?"

"You always wonder, you know," he said, shifting his gaze to the commotion on the other side of the window. "Hell, years later, I still see faces in my sleep. Of the men I served with. The ones I saw die and I ask myself...could I have done something different? Could I have changed that somehow?"

Was that all it was? she asked herself. Was Jericho haunted by the images of what might have been? Or was there more to it? Had he had the opportunity to save her brother? Her breath came faster now as she listened and, though she wasn't sure she wanted the answer, she had to ask the question.

"Why did Jericho think he could have saved Brant?"

The older man whipped his head around to meet her gaze, and he must have seen that she'd known nothing about this. That he'd told her something that Jericho had been keeping from her. And panic flickered briefly over his features before they once again became carefully blank.

"Uh," he said, setting the coffee mug down onto the counter. "Don't mind me, my mouth starts running, there's no telling what might come out of it. I better get out there, ride herd on those guys and make sure they're hammering everything together right."

"Sam…" She hopped off the high kitchen stool and stared at him. Her heartbeat was staggering wildly, as if it couldn't quite find the regular rhythm. Her breath was whooshing in and out of her lungs and her mind was screaming. It was all she could do to keep her voice low and controlled. "Tell me. Did Jericho let my brother die?"

"No, he did not," the older man said tightly. "But I can see I spoke out of turn. Whatever else happened is for Jericho to tell or not as he sees fit. I admire you a lot, Daisy. But this is not my story to tell. Now, excuse me, I'm going back to work."

Stunned, she simply stood there, speechless. What did it mean? Was this the secret Jericho had been keeping from her? What had happened on the day Brant died? What was Jericho hiding?

Alone in the bright, cheerful kitchen, with sunlight pooling all around her, Daisy felt as if she were at the bottom of a deep, dark hole.

Sam would have been surprised to know that Jericho hadn't gone to the high country at all. Instead, he'd steered his Jeep down the mountain and had driven directly to Justice's ranch. He'd needed to talk to somebody, to try to straighten out everything that was in his head and he had known that Justice would talk straight and say exactly what he was thinking—whether Jericho liked it or not.

"You really are an idiot, aren't you?" Justice shook his head in disgust and took a long drink of his beer.

"Thanks. Now I remember why I came to

you." Jericho jumped up from his chair and stalked the perimeter of the ranch office. He'd always liked this room. It was purely masculine and the one spot Justice had been able to defend from Maggie's influences. Every other inch of the ranch had been transformed or redecorated, but here, Justice drew a line.

Jericho slapped one hand on the fireplace mantel, looked over his shoulder at his brother and said, "You wouldn't be mad?"

"Hell, yes, I'd have been mad." Justice lifted his booted feet to the corner of the desk and crossed them at the ankle. "I *was* mad when Maggie showed up with Jonas in her arms and claimed he was mine."

"He is yours."

"Yeah, but I didn't believe her."

"So who's the idiot?" Jericho countered.

"You are. I'm a recovering idiot. There's a difference."

"Damn it, Justice," he complained. "She seduced me for my sperm!"

"Sneak up on you in the night, did she?"

"Not funny."

A short bark of laughter shot from his brother's throat and had Jericho scowling at him. "The hell it's not. You can't be seduced if you're not willing. And if you're so damned protective of your sperm, why didn't you have the little suckers corraled?"

He didn't have an answer for that one, so he turned around, stared into the dancing flames in the hearth and tried not to grind his own teeth into powder.

"You're not listening," he ground out. "She tricked me. Right from the beginning. Lied to me. Used me."

"Yeah, well, welcome to the world. People lie sometimes." Justice took another drink of his beer, balanced the can atop his flat abdomen and reminded his brother, "But when it mattered, when it really counted, she told you the truth. Besides, if you're looking for perfection, Jericho, you're not gonna find it."

"Yeah, she did," he agreed, remembering the look on her face when she'd told him. When she'd seen his reaction. Well, damn it, he'd like to know what man would have reacted differently. "I never planned on a family, you know," he said, talking to himself as much as Justice. "Wife. Kids. I never wanted anyone so dependent on me that my death could destroy them. I never wanted to cause anyone that kind of pain."

"Just *this* kind of pain then?" Justice argued. "That girl loves you, Jericho. She's carrying your baby and she loves you and you walked out. You turned tail and ran out the minute she really needed you. The minute you were actually tested."

Well, that didn't set well with him. He hadn't thought of his leaving in those specific terms. But now that he had, he was forced to admit that Justice was right. He'd walked out not only on the woman he loved, but on his own child, too. What did that say about a man's honor?

"There's something else to think about, too," Justice said. "Didn't you tell me that there was something you hadn't told *her?*"

That brought him up short. In all the mess with Daisy and his fury at her deception, he hadn't stopped to consider that he'd been keeping secrets, too. *And if you're keeping secrets, isn't that the same damn thing as lying?*

Hell.

"So maybe, Jericho," his brother mused aloud, "it's time to swallow that damn pride of yours, go home and talk to the woman you love before you do something so stupid she gets away from you altogether."

Daisy should have left.

She knew it.

Staying at Jericho's house only made his absence tear at her even harder. But how could she leave before she faced him? How could she go on with her life until she knew exactly what it was he'd been keeping from her?

How could she go on with her life without him?

That was the real question and one she didn't have an answer to.

She'd buried her emotions in cooking. There were now so many casseroles, desserts and stews stored in the freezers, no one at the camp would have to shop for supper for two years at least. And still, she was unsettled.

Nikki was on the couch beside her, curled into a ball, when suddenly she jumped straight up, gave a loud, sharp bark and jumped to the floor. Her nails clattered on the wood planks as she raced to the front door.

Daisy's insides twisted into knots as she stood up. Jericho was home. At last.

The door swung open, but Daisy stood her ground and listened as Jericho's deep voice rumbled out.

"Missed me, huh?" he asked and Nikki's soft whines answered him. "Yeah," he said, "crazy thing is, I missed you, too, CB."

Confused, Daisy frowned slightly and the frown was still on her face when he walked into the great room with Nikki held against his chest.

"Hi," he said.

"Hi yourself," she said, then asked, "What's CB?"

He shrugged, patted the little dog's head, then set her onto the floor where she ran circles around him. "Coyote Bait."

"Not very nice," she told him.

"She doesn't seem to mind."

He walked farther into the room and it occurred to her that they were behaving like polite strangers. A corner of her heart ached for what they'd lost.

"How are you?" he asked. "How is the baby?"

"We're both fine. You?"

"Same."

He scrubbed one hand across his jaw, something Daisy had noticed he did whenever he was stalling, looking for the right words to say.

So she waited to hear what he would come up with.

"You pissed me off," he finally said. "But I guess you figured that out."

"Yes, though you hid your feelings so cleverly, I deduced it when you left and didn't come back."

"Right." He nodded. "I shouldn't have done that. And so you know, it didn't do any good anyway because I took you with me when I left."

"Jericho—" Daisy started.

"No, don't say anything." He walked toward her and stopped just a few feet from her. "Not until I've told you something I should have told you long ago."

She swayed a little, then locked her knees to keep herself standing. This was what she'd been waiting for. What she'd been dreading. What had kept her dreams filled with images of her lost brother, tangling with visions of Jericho and all he'd come to mean to her. Now she was both terrified of learning the truth and determined to hear it.

"You mean about Brant's death?"

Surprise flickered in his eyes. "What do you know about that?"

"Not enough," she said. "Sam—"

"Damn it."

"Don't you be mad at him," she said quickly. "He thought you'd already told me whatever it is that you're keeping from me and when he realized you hadn't, he wouldn't say anymore."

Outside, night was falling and the setting sun was painting the sky in brilliant colors. Crimson-stained clouds studded the horizon and Daisy realized a storm was brewing. Well, that was appropriate because another kind of storm was building right here.

"What happened to my brother?" she demanded, moving right up to him, fixing her eyes on his. "How did he really die?"

Pain shot across his eyes, but Daisy wouldn't be moved. She had to know. Was she in love with a man who was the cause of her brother's death? Had she created a child with a man she should hate?

"You know how he died," Jericho said softly, staring into her eyes.

"I don't know why."

"Ah, hell." Jericho peeled off the worn brown leather bomber jacket he habitually wore and tossed it onto the couch. He wore a red T-shirt with the words *King Adventure* stenciled on the left breast pocket. Folding his arms across his chest, he braced his feet in a wide stance and said, "All right. Here we go." Watching her as if he couldn't bear to look away, he said, "Brant volunteered for a dangerous mission and I could have stopped him from going."

"He volunteered?"

"Yeah." Now it was as if he couldn't stand still. He walked past her to the hearth, then turned around and came right back again.

He looked at her, but Daisy thought he was

really looking into the past. A past that was haunting them both.

"He knew it was dangerous. The captain called for volunteers and Brant's hand shot up." He smiled in memory and shook his head. "The kid knew no fear. He was eager to serve. Proud to serve."

"Yes, he was," Daisy said and nearly sighed with relief as the knots inside her began to loosen. She couldn't say why because she didn't know the whole truth yet, but looking up at Jericho now, she knew with a bone-deep certainty that this man would have done anything to keep her brother safe. There was simply no way he could have been responsible for Brant's death.

"And why do you think you should have stopped him?"

"Because he was a kid," Jericho snapped irritably. "Sure of himself and not cocky with it either, but he was just a damn kid."

Her brother's face rose up in her mind and

Daisy saw what Jericho was obviously not seeing. Her brother had been young, yes. Too young to die and, God, she would always wish that he'd come home, married, had had a family and lived to be a cranky old man. But that hadn't happened, so she would deal with reality.

What she wouldn't do was take away from her brother's sacrifice by playing 'what if?'

"I could have stopped him," Jericho muttered thickly, spearing his gaze into hers. "Could have gone to the captain, recommended he choose someone else. Done…something."

"I have one question, Jericho, and I want you to give me your gut reaction answer, okay?"

"Yeah. What is it?"

"Was Brant ready for that mission? Trained? Capable?"

"Absolutely," he said without hesitation.

And the last of the knots inside her fell free. Daisy took a deep breath, sighed it out and moved toward the man she loved to distraction.

Reaching up, she laid one hand on his cheek and said, "Then you have nothing to regret."

"But—"

"You know, it's ironic," Daisy told him thoughtfully. "I raised him, and you're the one who made him into a man. Yet you're the one thinking of him as a boy."

Jericho's jaw dropped and his eyes went wide. A hundred different emotions chased each other across his face as seconds ticked past.

"It wasn't your fault, Jericho," she whispered, leaning into him, willing him to believe her. "Brant made his choices. He was a Marine and he took the same chances any of you did. You can't take that away from him now by putting the blame for his death on yourself."

"You surprise me. Endlessly," he said.

"Good." She smiled. "I understand how you feel, believe me. But you could have told me this before."

He grabbed her and yanked her close. He dipped his head, buried his face in the curve of her neck and inhaled her scent as if he were taking one long, last breath. "I've carried that around with me for so long…"

"Time to let it go. Time to think about the future, not the past."

"Our future," he said, lifting his head to kiss her once, twice. He threaded his fingers through her hair, skimmed his gaze over her face as though he were burning her image into his brain. "I love you, Daisy. I want you. I want our baby."

"Jericho…"

"Stay, Daisy," he said. "Marry me and stay."

She sighed, smiled and whispered, "Okay."

Epilogue

One month later...

"You noticed it's snowing, right?"

Jericho grinned at his wife and pulled her up close to him. "Yeah, I noticed. Pretty, isn't it?"

It really was. Their campsite was alongside the lake and the snow was falling in huge, soft tufts. Silence reigned in the white darkness and the only sound came from their whispered conversation and the hiss and snap of their fire.

"Gorgeous. And cold," Daisy said, burrowing

in even closer. "Don't forget cold." She turned her face up to his. "Tell me again why we're taking a honeymoon camping trip in late October?"

"To be alone," he reminded her, using one hand to toss another piece of wood on the campfire in front of them. "Most of the King family is still at the lodge. My family doesn't like leaving a good party in a hurry. Some of them will probably still be there when we get back."

"I like them all."

"Yeah," he said, "me, too. But I'm just as glad they're not here at the moment."

"True."

Nikki hadn't been happy about being left behind, but she was so busy being spoiled by Bella, Daisy didn't think the little dog would miss them for long. Besides, this trip was about them. Newlyweds. That word made her smile. Behind them, a tent stood, waiting for them to snuggle in and Jericho had already told her of his plans for just how to spend their first night on the trail.

"Hotels are nice, too," she whispered, then sighed as he skimmed his fingers across the tip of her nipple. Even through the heavy sweater she wore, she felt the heat of his touch and knew she'd have gone anywhere with him.

"Our first 'date' was at a campfire, remember?" he teased.

"Some date. You were trying to get rid of me."

"Nope, I was trying to keep my hands off you," he confessed. "Now, I don't have to."

Daisy looked at her gold wedding band in the firelight and when it winked at her, she smiled in appreciation. "It was a nice wedding, wasn't it?"

He sighed, dropped his forehead to hers and said, "Yeah, yeah, it was. Almost worth what you, Maura, Maggie and Bella put us all through for the past month getting the camp ready for the wedding."

Daisy laughed and snaked both arms around his middle. "Almost? Almost?"

Jericho grinned at her and couldn't imagine his life without her. She'd brought him closer to his family. She'd eased his mind, his heart, and she'd opened up his soul to the possibilities of real love. He'd spend the rest of his life thanking whatever kind fates had sent her to him.

"Definitely worth it," he amended.

"Oh, and Maggie told me that Justice has some ideas about how we can open up the camp to inner-city kids…"

Yep, she'd brought a lot of changes, he thought and smiled as he watched her animated features brightening at the idea of a new challenge. She was the perfect woman for him. If he could just get her to stop talking.

Being a military man, he used diversionary tactics, sliding one hand up under the hem of her sweater to cup her breast.

"Oh, my…"

"Talk later?"

"You bet. But, Jericho," she sighed as he

stroked his thumb across her nipple, "there's just one more thing you should know about me."

"Hmm? What's that?"

"I really don't like camping," she whispered.

"Bet I can change your mind," he said, smiling against her mouth.

"I don't think so…"

He shifted, drawing her into the privacy of their tent, lifting the hem of her sweater and gliding his mouth along her skin to the swell of her breast.

"Okay," she admitted, "maybe you can change my mind…"

* * * * *